HACKER REVELATION

WHITE HAT SECURITY, BOOK 5

LINZI BAXTER

Hacker Revelation
White Hat Security Series, Book 5
Copyright © 2018 by Linzi Baxter
Kindle Edition
Editor: Jennifer Wadsworth, Red Adept Editing
Cover Artist: Cassy Roop, Pink Ink Designs

All rights reserved. Except for use in any review, the reproduction or utilization of this work, in whole or in part, in any form by any electronic, mechanical, or other means now known or hereafter invented, is forbidden without permission of the author.

The unauthorized reproduction or distribution of this copyrighted work is illegal. Criminal copyright infringement (including infringement without monetary gain) is investigated by the FBI and is punishable by up to five years in federal prison and a fine of $250,000.

Please purchase only authorized electronic editions, and do not participate in or encourage the electronic piracy of copyrighted materials. Your support of the author's rights is appreciated.

This is a work of fiction. Names, characters, businesses, places, events, and incidents are either the products of the author's imagination or used in a fictitious manner. Any resemblance to actual persons, living or dead, or actual events is purely coincidental.

BLURB

Romance never dies...

Kat and Antonio Ross seemed to have their whole lives ahead of them. Six years ago, they married each other. But the next day turned to tragedy when Kat and Antonio were led to believe the other died in a violent shootout. Since then, they've led separate lives. Kat began working for her uncle, the CIA director, as an assassin. Antonio, an ex-Navy SEAL, started a well-respected mercenary company.

But when Antonio finds out Kat is alive, he brings her back home. He wants her to quit the CIA for the sake of their child. Kat agrees and starts working at a women's shelter, where an abused woman seeks her help. Kat's instincts kick in, and she's back to making enemies again. And when the woman's husband comes after her, it's just the beginning of this heart-pounding thrill ride.

Hacker Revelation is a fast-paced and sexy novel full of romantic suspense. Kat and Antonio have the chance to live the quiet life. But life's never been quiet for these two. And when the chips are down and their whole lives are at stake, nothing's ever going to stop them. Because love is in the air… and so are the bullets.

ACKNOWLEDGMENTS

I would like to express my gratitude to the many people who saw me through this book: My editor, Jennifer, who did an amazing job and worked hard to help me craft a better story. Cassy for doing an astounding job with the cover art. Michelle and Jean for taking the time to beta read for me. My husband and family for always being there to support me. This book couldn't have happened without all of you!

Thank you to all you amazing readers who are going on this journey alongside me. I hope *Hacker Revelation* is all that you hoped for and more!

1

ANTONIO

"Mommy... can't... breathe," Antonio Jr. choked out. Kat had her arms wrapped tight around his little body, and tears streamed down her face. When Kat didn't loosen her hold, I bent down next to her and placed my hand on her back. Her eyes shifted toward me, and she mouthed, "Thank you."

Kat needed to learn that I would do anything for her and our son.

"Kitty Kat, can I get a hug from our son?" She nodded and slowly released him. Ant jumped into my arms, and it took everything in me to hold back my tears. When the school had called earlier to inform us that they couldn't find Ant, fear had coursed through my body. I was feeling the effect of the unused adrenaline now that Ant had been found.

I pulled back and stared down at my son. He wore

a *Cars* T-shirt that matched his blue shorts, and his little lip quivered. "Did I do something wrong, Daddy?"

But I couldn't answer him. I still didn't know why Ant had hidden in the janitor's closet.

"Can we move this to my conference room? The afternoon bell will ring soon," Principal Anderson said.

I nodded.

Principal Anderson was in her early thirties. Her mouse-brown hair was in a bun, and black-framed glasses sat low on her nose. Her six-inch heels added height to her small frame. She was pretty but bland compared to my firecracker of a wife.

Ant put one tiny hand in mine and grabbed Kat's with the other. I met Kat's eyes over Ant, and she gave me a watery smile. We followed Principal Anderson as her high heels clicked across the white floor.

A memory flashed through my brain of the last time I had been ordered to the principal's office. I was in middle school, and Asher thought it would be funny if we replaced the science teacher's dead frogs with live ones. When the teacher opened the pail of frogs to hand them out to students for dissection, they all escaped. We got expelled from school for a week, and Mom made us help the house cleaner the whole time.

Principal Anderson opened the door that led to her conference room. She sat down at the child-size table. I eyed the table and tried to figure out how I would fold my six-foot-three frame into a two-foot chair. Kat and Ant grabbed the two red seats and sat with ease, leaving a yellow chair for me. I decided not to burden the tiny chair and leaned against the wall instead.

In a soft voice, Principal Anderson asked, "Antonio, can you explain to your parents and me why you hid from your teachers today?"

Ant swung his eyes in my direction, seeking my okay. I nodded.

"Daddy said if I saw Uncle Juan, I was supposed to hide." Ant picked up the crayon on the table and started to draw on the piece of paper in front of him.

Kat let out a gasp, then she pulled the piece of paper away from Ant to get his full attention. "Are you sure it was Uncle Juan? Sometimes we make mistakes and think we see something we didn't."

I believed Ant. I took my phone from my pocket and sent Asher a text to have someone pull all the video feed from around the school. Asher was my twin brother and co-owner of our security firm, AA Security. Earlier in the day, we had been under the impression that Juan Sanchez, Ant's uncle, had planted a bomb in Kat's sister's car. SWAT had spent the morning defusing the bomb.

"Duh, Mom. I know who Uncle Juan is."

Kat sent me a worried look.

I bent down to Ant's level. "Can you tell me specifically what happened?"

Ant let out an aggravated sigh. "Kurt and I were playing ball. When Kurt threw the ball wide, it went by the fence. Uncle Juan was at the fence, but he couldn't get in. He told me that Aunt Sophie was in the hospital, and I needed to go with him. But I knew he was lying. If Aunt Sophie were hurt, you would come get me. So I did what you said, Dad. You told me if I ever saw Uncle Juan, I should hide, and you would find me. Did I do good?"

I scooped Ant into my arms and pressed a kiss against his head. "You did perfect." I sat Ant back in his chair next to his mom.

"Can I have ice cream, then?"

Everyone let out a chuckle at Ant's question. It helped relieve some of the tension in the room.

Principal Anderson cleared her throat. She had a No. 2 pencil in her hand, and she had taken notes on everything that was said. "Are the other kids in danger? This Juan character—is he bad news?"

How could I explain that the man after my family was the corrupt former director of the CIA? He was the number-one most-wanted terrorists in the world, with a $25 million reward for his capture. The number-two most-wanted terrorist was the leader of Al Qaeda.

"I think it would be better if we pull—"

Ant cut off my words with his own. "I want to stay here." His lip quivered.

I lowered myself to Ant's height. His steely gray eyes gazed back at me. No matter how many times I had looked at Ant in the last few weeks, it punched me in the gut every time I realized how much he looked like me.

"Buddy, I'm not saying you can't come back, but let's take you out for a week. I need you to stay with your grandparents."

"Okay. Grandma Ross always has warm cookies for me."

Cookies. Too bad adults weren't that easy to bribe. Kat could have bribed me with sex, and I would have dropped to her feet. I shook my head to get the image of Kat's naked body out of my mind.

She gave me a raised eyebrow in response to my far-off gaze as she rose from the child-sized chair.

I gathered Ant into my arms. "I'm sorry Ant worried you today. I hope you will allow him to come back once his uncle is behind bars."

Principal Anderson gazed past us, lost in her own thoughts. "I understand things happen in our lives. We would love to have Ant back when his uncle is in jail." She ruffled Ant's hair and extended her hand. "Thank you for understanding that I need to protect all the students."

Ant's school had dismissed the students for the day. Only the teachers remained. Mrs. Ferguson, Ant's teacher, gave him a hug and had tears in her eyes when we went to say good-bye.

The walk to the car was uneventful. Kat lifted Ant into his car seat and kissed him on the forehead. She mumbled something to him that I couldn't hear. Ant leaned in and kissed his mom on the cheek before I closed his door and followed Kat around the car. It had been a difficult couple of hours, so I wrapped my arms around Kat. She automatically rested her head on my shoulder. Her eyes still had a sheen of water.

"He's fine, Kitty Kat."

"I'm still worried." Her words came out muffled against my chest.

We had almost made it to the house when Ant asked the question I had hoped to avoid. "Did you track me with ESP?"

I let out a chuckle. "GPS, son. Yes. You did good. I'm so proud of you."

Kat was deadly quiet in the passenger seat. The tension in the cab was almost suffocating.

"Do you have GPS devices on anyone else besides our son?"

Six years earlier, Kat and I had run an undercover

operation for Juan Sanchez. It was the first and last case we worked together. That was when Juan was the director of the CIA. I fell for the fiery redhead the second she stormed into the briefing room and commanded everyone's attention. By the end of the week, I had my ring on her finger. It was a whirlwind romance.

The op was informal, and we had the intel we needed by the following week, so we spent an extra day in Berlin to celebrate our wedding. The morning of our flight home, we stopped in Kat's favorite café to have coffee. We had just sat down when someone fired on the restaurant with automatic weapons. I took three shots before I could grab my gun.

When I woke in the hospital, Juan Sanchez informed me that Kat had been shot and didn't survive surgery. I had lived the last five and a half years thinking my wife was dead. Those days were my darkest. The sun never seemed to rise. Many nights, I wished I would have died with her. She was my sunshine.

When Sophie, a close friend of my sister-in-law's, was escorted out of White Hat Security by the CIA agent Zane, I had used my connection to find out why they had taken her. Juan, who happened to be Sophie's uncle, had been forcing her to work for the CIA. During the briefing I barged in on, an analyst had a picture of Sophie's sister in a case file. Juan tried to prevent Sophie from seeing it, but it didn't work, and I saw it as well. Sophie's sister was my dead wife, who wasn't dead after all.

After a carefully planned mission to find and extract her, I finally held my wife in my arms for the first time in almost six years.

So yes, I had bugged her. What sane man wouldn't have?

"Kitty K—"

"Don't you fucking 'Kitty Kat' me, Antonio. Did you put a tracking device on me?"

Our little man with big ears picked up everything. "Mommy said a bad word."

Kat rested her head in her hands. "I'm sorry, Ant. You're right. We don't say those words."

I had to hold back the chuckle. Kat cursed all the time, but lately, she had tried to cut back on the swear words. A few more would fly when I admitted I bugged her shoes.

"I lost you once. It will not happen again. For every one you remove, I will replace it with two. Don't try me on this, Kat."

"It's okay, Mommy. We are a cool blue dot on Uncle Asher's computer."

Kat looked back at our son and let out an aggravated sigh. "It would've been nice to know. Do you have a GPS tracker in your shoes, Antonio?"

"Yes."

Kat's head whipped in my direction. She hadn't expected me to say yes. Juan Sanchez wasn't the only dangerous case we had. Every member of my team wore a GPS device. Asher and his fiancé, CJ, were the only two people who had access to the GPS information.

"Oh."

It wasn't often that I shocked Kat out of a lecture. I reached across the center console, grabbed her hand, brought it up to my lips, and kissed it. She didn't fight me at all.

"Kat, everyone on my team, including me, wears GPS trackers. Our team takes on dangerous cases, so Asher and I decided to make sure each team member was protected. Many of our significant others and the people we are protecting wear them as well. I don't want to lose anyone, especially you and Ant, again. I knew you would protest, so I put the devices in your shoes. It took me a few days, since you have close to a hundred pairs. Are you still mad at me?"

"No, but I wish you would have let me know. Can we stop and pick up dinner? I'm not in the mood to cook."

Asher had texted me when we were at the school. He and CJ were bringing dinner over along with the video CJ pulled from the area around the school. CJ was my brother Asher's fiancé. About a year ago, Asher had told the family he was gay. CJ was a perfect partner for my brother.

"Asher's bringing food. Do you want to call Sophie and see if she and Zane want to come over for dinner?"

Kat tried Sophie, but she didn't answer. I wasn't surprised. She and Zane had finally made up after a month of putting each other through hell.

When we got home, Asher and I spent the night analyzing the video. The video confirmed Ant's story that Juan had been at the school. We used satellite surveillance to follow his car. He had pulled into a public parking lot. I asked my newest hire, Jacob, to go to the parking garage and report back what he found.

He later sent me a text saying Juan's car was parked in the back of the garage and wiped down. Juan had escaped our grasp again, and we were back to square one.

2

KAT

For the last few weeks, I had been working on changing my life and had enjoyed every moment.

The biggest change was learning not to kill first and ask questions later. If Antonio ever found out about the alligator in our backyard to whom I'd fed a few bodies over the last few weeks, he would put me on house arrest.

Since my retirement from the CIA as their top assassin, I had volunteered at the Ross Women's Outreach Center. The Ross Family Foundation ran the center and worked to eliminate domestic violence. It felt good to give back to society. It was also one of the hardest jobs I had ever experienced.

Each day, I saw women come in with black-and-blue eyes or cracked ribs. The women at the center dealt not only with physical abuse but mental abuse as well. Some women had lived on the streets for years, waiting for a spot to open at the center.

Each of the volunteers helped in different areas of the center. I assisted the women working on their GED. I also planned to run a self-defense class in the next few days.

Lily, one of the women I'd met, had been in and out of the center for the past two years. She still lived with her abusive husband. During the day, she came to the center to work on getting her GED. Each day, I discussed with her the options she had for leaving her abusive husband. Lily reminded me of a Victoria's Secret model, but years of abuse had made sure she couldn't see her own beauty or worth.

"How are you doing today, Lily?" When I wrapped my arms around her to give her a hug, I noticed she flinched as I touched her back.

I saw red. The need to find the man who hurt her was at the forefront of my mind. I wanted to demand answers and ask if she had called the police. But that wasn't the best way to approach abused women.

Lily had gotten pregnant her last year of high school. When her parents found out, they kicked her out of their house. Her father was a minister, and her mother worked for the church. They said she had embarrassed her family's name.

After her parents disowned her, she turned to her then-boyfriend and father of her child. She and her child had lived with him off and on for the past six years. When the beatings became too much, she would find shelter.

I'd been trying to get information about her husband or where they lived. If she didn't give me the info soon. I was going to follow her home some night. Not in a creepy, serial-killer way, though. At least, not for her.

"I'm okay. I need to study for my GED. I'm taking the test tomorrow."

Lily's son, Tommy, was the reason she fought for a better life. "Mom's going to pass the test. Then we'll move away from Greg."

A shadow came across Lily's face. I needed to figure out a way to protect Lily and Tommy or eliminate Greg. Antonio kept telling me I couldn't help everyone. But over the last two weeks, I'd become close to Lily. We had formed a bond instantly, and she was part of my family now. I would do anything to protect her and her son.

I took a seat at the round table and joined Lily and Tommy. "You're right. Your mom will pass tomorrow. You know why your mom is going to pass?"

The little man climbed into his mother's lap. Her

wince of pain didn't go unnoticed. "Duh. Everyone knows. My mommy is the smartest."

"*You're* so smart," I told him. "I bet you will be a doctor when you grow up."

"Nope. A policeman to protect my mommy from bad men."

Those words broke my heart, and when I looked up, Lily's eyes had a sheen to them. I thought Tommy might like to spend time with Antonio and Asher at AA Security. The little man would enjoy being told stories about the bad guys they had taken down. He would also get to spend time with good role models.

"You will make an awesome police officer." I pointed to the group of kids that played in the corner of the room. The center had added an area with toys and a jungle gym inside so the mothers could work on studies and keep an eye on their kids. I had learned that women who were abused at home didn't like their kids being out of sight. "Why don't you go play with Chance while I talk to your mommy?"

Tommy jumped off Lily's lap and ran toward his friends.

When the little man reached the jungle gym, I asked my burning question. "Now, tell me why you are walking with a limp, favoring your left side, and wincing when someone touches you?"

"How can you tell?"

"I have a skill set."

She let out a sigh before answering. "Everyone around here talks about their past except you. How did you get this skill set? Were you a cop?"

I'd been asked many times about my past. It had become a joke. I made up a new story each time I was asked, and now everyone wanted to hear what the next story would be. The kids loved to hear the stories I made up. The previous day, I had told them I was an ex-circus clown on the run. The foundation didn't ask questions because Alexander Ross Sr. had brought me to the center and told everyone I was a new volunteer. Alexander Sr. was Antonio's dad, and everyone at the clinic adored him.

Something about Lily made me want to tell her the truth, but we needed to get her help first. "Stop changing the subject and answer the question."

"Tommy was having a hard time sleeping. Greg was supposed to be at wor—" Lily reached up and covered her eyes. The sound of her sob made my anger rise. "He got fired. Said it was my fault."

Any man that blamed the mother of his child for being fired deserved a slow, painful death. It looked like Betty and I were going hunting again. Betty was my sniper rifle. On second thought, Greg didn't deserve a quick death. He deserved to be tortured for hours.

There was no way Antonio would let me turn the basement into a torture chamber, so I mentally made a list of items I would need for a storage locker. My loving husband wanted me to acclimate myself back into society after being a world-renowned assassin. I didn't think it was fair that Antonio still got to hunt people down and take them out.

"Did you go to the hospital to make sure you were okay?"

"Yeah. I have a broken rib. The doctor said it will heal in time."

Lily needed to find another place to stay. She used the outreach center for help with her GED, but she didn't feel it was appropriate to take a bed when so many women lived on the street.

"You can't go home. I'm having one of Antonio's men pick you up and take you to a safe house until we figure something else out."

The look on Lily's face told me all I needed to know. She hadn't planned to leave Greg. Many women stayed in abusive relationships because of fear or because they thought it was normal. Deep down in my gut, I felt Lily stayed because she didn't think she could do any better. Years of being belittled had taken a drastic toll on her self-esteem.

"No!" she shouted. "He will hurt your friends."

At her shout, everyone's attention zeroed in on us. I

waited for everyone in the room to go back to their conversations before I said, "I've taken on men ten times worse than Greg, and so has my husband's staff."

"So you've said."

I ignored her remark and changed the subject. "I want to see if any of you ladies want to take a self-defense course. I can teach it in the craft room if we move the tables."

Lily's shoulders tensed at my words.

"If the violence is too much, I understand. You ladies mean so much to me. I want you to have all the things necessary to take care of yourself. But I understand if it is too violent."

"No, I want to learn on one condition. Tell me who taught you. I think you came here to heal something yourself, and if you don't talk about it, you won't be able to."

My story was so messed up that I highly doubted she would believe it. Over the years, I've made a lot of enemies who tricked me into thinking they were on my side. It was hard to trust people, but something about Lily made it easy to trust her. Deep down, I knew she wouldn't betray me. She reminded me a lot of my sister's friends, Bridget and Jessica.

I took a deep breath. "You won't believe me."

"Try me."

"I'm a retired assassin for the CIA."

Lily laughed so hard that she winced from the pain. "Oh my god, that is so funny." When she noticed I hadn't laughed, she sobered up quickly. "You're serious?"

"I said you wouldn't believe me. But I've left the life behind."

"Umm, can you do that?"

Most people in my position didn't leave the CIA. They worked the job until they died or were eliminated. CIA agents were bred to protect the country, but Juan had forced me into it. I loved doing the work to protect the nation and our freedom, but it was so lonely, and I missed the family I had lost. While I was working for the CIA, I didn't know they were still alive or I would have left earlier.

Zane, Sophie's boyfriend, was President Zack Tucker's brother. It wasn't Zane that called him, though. My husband did it. Antonio called the president of the United States and demanded he let me retire from the CIA. I was a little mad at Antonio for demanding I leave the only job I knew, but I understood where his demand came from. He had lost me once to the corruption in the government, and he wouldn't let it happen again.

Zack had asked to speak to me before giving Antonio his answer. Over the years, I had met the president a few times when I was briefed on cases.

"POTUS allowed me to retire. I decided to take him up on the offer. I wanted to give back and help people in need."

"POTUS?"

"President Zack Tucker."

"You've met the president of the United States?"

Zack and Zane were two of the nicest men I knew. It had taken Zane a little while to get off his ass and go after my sister. He was pigheaded. Zack ordered Zane to clean up the CIA. Last I had heard, POTUS wanted Zane to take over the director position.

"Sure. My sister is engaged to his brother Zane."

A loud scream interrupted our conversation, and we both looked toward the children's play area. One of the kids had tripped on a toy fire truck and fell. Tommy and his friend played on the other side with a couple trucks.

Seeing that Tommy was all right, Lily looked back at me with wonder in her eyes. "I want your life. You are the most fascinating person I've ever met."

On the outside, the life of an assassin sounded cool, but it was extremely lonely. But I hadn't had a choice. Juan had threatened the only thing I cared about. Antonio Jr. was my life, and if keeping him safe meant I had to keep doing what Juan asked, I did. In the end, I got my husband and sister back, so maybe the years of loneliness had been worth what I had now.

In two months, it would be Antonio Jr.'s birthday. It was the first we'd get to spend with my family. The more I thought about it, the more I realized I had a perfect life, and I wouldn't go back to change anything.

"You have an amazing boy, and you're working on your GED. I've no doubt you are going places. We all need help from time to time."

"When was the last time you leaned on someone?"

I grabbed the piece of paper in front of me and tore it into pieces. Thinking about the call we got from Ant's school yesterday reminded me how I leaned on Antonio. "Our son went missing yesterday. Someone is after my sister and me and would use my son to get to us. I leaned on my husband, Antonio, for help."

If it hadn't been for Antonio, I might have lost my mind. At the school, he maintained a calm demeanor and ordered people to do what he needed. When I learned he had put a tracking device in our son's sneakers, I was angry that he had hidden something so important from me but happy, too, because we had found our son so easily.

Antonio admitted he put a tracker in my shoes, too, so when we arrived home, I checked the inside of my shoes and found the device. I had agreed to keep it in place until we found Juan. Once Juan Sanchez was six feet underground or in the tummy of the alligator I kept fed, I'd be ditching the tracker.

Lily grabbed the pencil from the table and pulled out her study materials. "That is one thing I will never do—lean on a man for help."

"Well, you are going to lean today. One of Antonio's men will pick you up. You need time to heal. Not all men are like Greg. Let's get you back on your feet, and then we can find someone for you."

"Nope. Never going to date again. Tommy is the only man I need."

After I thought Antonio had been shot and killed in the cafe, I closed my heart to love. I knew what true love was and thought I couldn't feel for anyone else what I felt for Antonio. Lily, on the other hand, had dealt with an evil bastard. She didn't understand true love and how to put all your trust in one person's hands.

Antonio's face flashed in my mind. "Closing your heart to love won't help. In time, you'll find a man you can trust."

"I'm worried I won't get to that place in my life. Greg is never going away." She shrugged her shoulders. "If I move on, he could hurt anyone I date. Why would I do that to someone?"

"Oh, honey. Don't worry about Greg. I will have Antonio and his team look into him. We will make sure nothing happens to you."

"I don't have money to pay for his services."

"We aren't going to charge you." Lily didn't need to know that I would pay for the services. I had decided it was time I used my trust fund to help people. Juan had used it for years to destroy people's lives. It was time the money was used for good.

"I can't expect you to do that for free. When I find a job, I will pay him to help me."

"How many ways do I need to say this, Lily? We will not take your money. Have you ever heard of the Ross family?"

"Yes. Those people are rich. I believe they fund this outreach center. What does that have to do with anything?"

"I'm married to Antonio Ross. Yes, they are rich, and I have a lot of money of my own. We don't need you paying us. Let us help you. When you are on your feet, you can pay it forward."

Lily looked at me, appearing slightly stunned. "Fine."

"Okay, get back to studying. I'm going to talk to Lisa about setting up the class. I will be back tomorrow. Stay safe."

I reached into my pocket, pulled out my phone, and sent Antonio a text asking him to have one of his men pick up Lily and her son and take them to a safe house. His reply came back immediately, telling me Jacob would pick them up in an hour.

Jacob was one of the newer men that worked for Antonio. He had left the navy two months earlier. He was on the shy side and didn't talk much.

I went back to where Lily sat. "Lily, a man named Jacob will be here in one hour. He is your new bodyguard. Please don't give him any trouble." When it looked like she would argue, I held up my hand. "Please let me do this, if not for you, then for Tommy."

She shook her head, stood up, and wrapped me in a hug. "You are an amazing woman."

Lily went back to her table to study. I felt the weight of the world lift from my shoulders, knowing Lily would be watched by one of Antonio's men. I was positive she would pass her GED tomorrow—she nailed every practice test she took—and the foundation would help her find a job.

I walked down the hall in the back of the building toward the shelter coordinator's office. The white walls were filled with artwork made by the kids that had passed through the shelter. The pictures showed such hope and happiness.

When I arrived at Lisa's office, the door was partially open. I knocked and pushed the door open. "Hey, Lisa. Do you have a second?"

Lisa Alvarez was in her late fifties. She had worked for the shelter since the day it opened. Lisa was nothing but positive with the women and kids that came through. She took the time to help everyone and make sure they were getting the best care she could offer.

"Sure. What can I do for you?"

"I was wondering if I could host a self-defense class for the ladies."

"Oh, we've wanted to do one for so long, but the shelter couldn't afford to bring in an instructor. Any tips you have for the ladies will help. You've done so much since you started volunteering. It means the world to these ladies."

I felt like I hadn't done enough. The classes would give these women a bit of a fighting chance, and it might help to boost their confidence.

"Thank you for letting me help and teach the class. I want to give back. I would like to start the classes this week if you could coordinate getting people to take them. Any day is fine for me to teach."

Lisa looked excited. "It sounds like a plan."

"After a few classes, I can bring some volunteer men." When Lisa looked like she would protest, I added, "I understand some of the women might shy away from them. But these are men I trust completely to help the women learn the best way to take them down. The women can practice on them."

Before I left, I let Lisa know about Lily and that I was hiring a bodyguard for her. Lisa told me I couldn't afford to fix every woman's problem, but she didn't know I had a billion dollars sitting in the bank or that I would use all the money to help these women get on their feet.

"Have a good night," I said to her on my way out.

3

ANTONIO

For the past month, I hadn't been able to keep the smile off my face. My dead wife was alive, and we had the most beautiful son. I couldn't remember how many nights I had lain in bed wishing for my wife back or wishing I had died in that café with her. When her face had appeared in that op folder, I thought I had lost my mind.

I was in the briefing room, and the men who sat around me would do anything I asked. For the past month, they had worked to track Juan Sanchez. Every time they got close, he slipped out of their hands. The bomb planted in Sophie's car was too much. We needed to get this guy off the streets.

"Sitrep," I barked.

The men in the room were used to my abrupt attitude, and that Juan was still on the loose had my nerves on end. I couldn't lose my wife again, and she was one of Juan's main targets. Thankfully, Kat trusted me to take care of the situation.

CJ leaned back in the chair opposite me. "Good morning to you too. I had hoped, since you were finally getting some, you would be a bit less brusque."

Asher and CJ had been living together for the past eight months, and a few weeks ago, Asher had finally proposed.

But CJ worked for White Hat Security, not AA Security. "Why are you here?"

Asher leaned forward in his leather chair. "Stop with the attitude. He's helping us with the Sanchez case."

I shook my head. "Sorry, CJ. I'm on my last nerve. We need to find this guy. I'm sick of looking over my shoulder."

The door to the conference room swung open, and Zane stepped in. Zane had started to work at AA Security a week ago. For the previous couple of months, he had helped his brother, President Zack Tucker, clean up the CIA. But Zane wanted to be close to his fiancée, Sophie, and that meant leaving the CIA. He also wanted to find Juan as badly as Kat and I did.

"Looking over your shoulder for what?"

"If you would show up to work on time, you would know," I snapped.

Zane lowered himself into the chair next to mine and picked up the operation file. "I'll ignore your attitude. Sophie is nervous about driving by herself, and that woman takes forever to get ready in the morning."

At Zane's words, guilt hit me in the chest. Zane wouldn't have been late for work if he didn't have a reason. Zane had mentioned the other day that Sophie still hadn't driven a car by herself since she'd been trapped in her car, sitting on top of a ticking bomb.

"You're right. You need to take care of Sophie. As I was telling these guys, I'm sick of Sanchez, and we need to take him down. I want him dead, and I don't care what your brother wants, even if he is the president of the United States. He needs to learn that some people are better dead than alive."

"I agree. Zack won't give the kill order even though he knows what happened with Sophie. There is no way I'm bringing the man in alive." There was no hesitation in Zane's voice. He and I were on the same page about Juan. We both planned to kill him and not turn him over.

"Okay, back to the case. What have we found?"

Asher said, "John sent over his preliminary report from the analysis he did on the bomb. He claims the detonator was constructed in a way he has only seen a couple times." Asher displayed a list of names on the projector. "Here is a list of the people I was planning on talking to."

I recognized none of the names on the list, and none of them were Russian. "Did John report anything else?"

Asher was tapping his pen on the table. "The bomb had dual trip switches. John has a call in to a couple people to see if they have any ideas."

Zane stood up. "We're chasing our tails, going after the bomb maker. Sanchez would've hired the job out. Knowing him, he's already eliminated the man who built and placed the bomb. Why are we not trying to find the fucker?" Zane was pacing back and forth. His anger at the situation was taking over. I understood. When I thought Juan had kidnapped Ant, I had almost lost it.

"This is our only lead," I replied. "We've had facial recognition software running on the NSA satellites and local traffic cameras. He's not leaving his house, or he has changed his face. Sanchez has been around long enough to know how we would track him and what we would use. The last sighting we have is three days ago at Ant's school. We tried to track that trail, and it went nowhere." Juan had showed his face that day because he wanted Ant to come with him. Luckily, my little man was smart enough to hide and ignore Juan's request.

CJ added, "I have every spare server White Hat has running to find Juan, and nothing has hit. I spent yesterday combing over the dark web message boards looking for anything leading to Sophie or Kat."

CJ had been working on the case since the beginning. He was good at working with computers. When the case was over, I planned on asking him to come work for AA Security. I needed to run the idea by Asher first, but I didn't think he would have a problem with it.

Zane took a sip of his coffee. "He won't look for people on the dark web. He'll look for people that owe him. I bet Sophie and Kat didn't get all the money he has."

"You going to tell Sophie and Kat they failed?"

"No. That stays in this room. I'm not saying they failed. Juan must have had cash hidden somewhere. Emergency funds. Everyone has a few million hid."

Leave it to a billionaire to think people hid a few million here and there. I knew everyone in our family had a few million hidden in different locations for emergency funds. Juan had been extremely rich at one time, when he was stealing money from Kat and Sophie's trust funds.

CJ looked around the table waiting for someone to correct Zane. "Umm, no. Most people don't hide a few million dollars. Don't know what world you live in."

"You're telling me none of you have money hid?" Zane asked.

Asher shrugged his shoulders. "I keep a few million hidden around. Juan's using hired guns from his past. We need to go back and look through Sophie and Kat's files."

"I have a copy of everything on my server," CJ said. "I think it would be better if I work on the case from here. If Sophie walks in on me looking at the files, she'll want to help."

I needed to send my sister-in-law Bridget, the owner of White Hat Security, a gift for allowing us to borrow one of her top hackers. When I finally stole him from her company, I would need more than a fruit basket, though.

"Does Bridget know why you're here?"

A blush crept across CJ's face. I knew he didn't like to lie to Bridget. She wasn't only his boss but a long-time friend. "No. Bridget would want to help too. I said you guys had a new drug trafficking case, and Asher needed help tracking someone's activity electronically."

CJ was right. She would want to be involved in the research. This case was dangerous, and Alex, my older brother, would have my head if I somehow put Bridget in the path of Juan's destruction. She was also six months pregnant with their second child.

"Were you able to go through the video feed from when the bomb was placed in Sophie's car?"

"A transformer blew around eight a.m.," CJ reported. "The power was out for two hours. I have a feeling that was when the bomb was planted. I combed through what video I had and saw no one near the car. White Hat Security has generators, so their power never went down, but Bridget only has cameras inside, not in the garage."

I remembered seeing a coffee shop next to White Hat Security. "The power was back up when we were working on the bomb. Did you go through the video during the time we were trying to disarm the bomb?"

"No. What do you want me to look for?" CJ asked.

I had to remind myself CJ was trained in pulling data, not in surveillance. He didn't have the skills to look through video and see a suspect watching the car. A high percentage of criminals came back and watched over their work.

"Anything out of the ordinary. Sanchez would want to know if he failed to eliminate Sophie. He was there, or he had someone watching." When CJ nodded his understanding, I added, "Give me an update later today. I'm looking through the files of possible new hires. The cases are piling up."

Zane glared at me, probably thinking we would drop the Sanchez case. But it was too close to home and would have all our attention until we took him down. Still, the calls for new cases kept pouring through the door.

"We're not dropping Sanchez. But I need to have someone work on the cases coming in."

I handed Zane, Asher, and CJ folders full of resumes. They were military men and women looking to leave when there term was up. CJ had a puzzled look on his face.

"CJ, I had planned to wait and talk to Asher to make sure he was okay with my idea. But I know my brother, and I know it's what he wants as well, so there's no reason to wait." When I looked in Asher's direction, he was shaking his head. He knew what I was going to ask. "Will you come work for us?"

The room was deadly quiet. All eyes were on CJ. I didn't know if he was excited or if he was trying to figure out how to say no.

CJ reached up and wiped his eyes. "Yes," he choked out.

Asher blew out a breath of relief. "Damn. For a minute, I thought you would say no."

CJ reached up and wiped his eyes again. "I love working here. Please don't tell Bridget that. We will tell her my Dom required me to work here."

"Not going to happen, love," Asher said with a

chuckle. "I'm scared of my brother's wife. We can tell her together. I think she will understand."

I really didn't want to be around for that conversation. Bridget would take it out on the people in the room, and I didn't want to be added to the no-fly list or be affected by whatever other evil electronic ways she used for revenge.

"Okay. One position filled. CJ, do in-depth backgrounds on all the men and women in those files. We need to hire at least six people."

I left the men in the conference room looking through the folder as I headed back to my office. I checked in with the temp office assistant.

"Good morning, Stacy."

She looked up from the report she was reading. "Good morning, Mr. Ross."

Stacy Carol was in her late twenties. She was on the shorter side, curvy, and had a feisty attitude. She fit in well with the team. Asher and I had hired her three months ago to be the administrative assistant for the office. Her contract was up at the end of the month, and if she wanted to stay, I would offer her a job.

"How many times do I have to tell you to call me Antonio? My father is Mr. Ross."

"What can I help you with, Mr. Ross?"

"You're fired."

She tilted her head as she decided how to answer

me. "You won't fire me. Here is your coffee from next door and your messages."

I grabbed the messages and coffee and headed to my office. AA Security was on the twenty-fourth floor of Ross Enterprise. Asher and I had opened the firm when we left the navy. My eldest brother owned Ross Enterprise, a high-end real estate firm. His office was one floor above Asher's and mine. It was nice being close to both of my brothers. Our youngest brother, Aaron, lived in Hollywood and was a hot-shot actor.

The stack of messages Stacy gave me was written on pink paper. The first message said a man named Zack had called but wouldn't leave a last name or phone number and seemed like a jackass. Stacy always wrote how she felt about the caller on the messages. I grinned. Stacy didn't realize she'd been talking to the president of the United States.

I dialed Zack's cell number from my desk phone. He answered immediately, and I could tell he was in a meeting because he excused himself from the room.

He got straight to the point. "Have you found him?"

I didn't need Zack breathing down my neck. "I will call you when we have Juan in custody." *Or dead*, I thought, but I wasn't going to tell Zack our plan.

Zack growled on the other side of the phone,

knowing what I had left unsaid. "You will not kill him. Bring him in alive."

"I'll call you the second we have something." I hung up the phone, not wanting any more shit from Zack. Something was going on with him, and if he wanted us to know, he would tell us.

I spent the rest of the day going over the reports on the cases we closed last week. We had three more cases come in—a sex-trafficking case, a bodyguard needed, and a cheating-husband case. I was sick of the cases where we were looking into cheating spouses. A knock on the door had me looking up.

Stacy stood with her purse in hand. "I'm heading out. You leaving soon?"

I glanced at the clock. It was time to go get Ant. Kat and I had decided to leave Ant in school. The Ross family donated millions over the years. AA Security installed the security system in the school. When I contacted the principal about Ant's return, she ran it by the other parents and agreed for us to add additional security. We didn't think Juan would strike the same place twice, but I had added additional security to the school, just in case. I grabbed my things and headed out to pick up my son.

"How was school today, little man?"

Ant climbed into his booster seat in the back of the

Range Rover. When I looked at him, I couldn't help feeling joyful.

"We had a real live police officer come to school."

Dread filled my stomach. "Why was an officer in your class?"

"He taught us Stranger Danger and how to call 9-1-1."

It sounded like a planned visit. That was a relief. "What should you do if a stranger walks up to you?"

Ant was going to the same preschool Asher and I had gone to. It was a private school near our neighborhood. They had good security and great teachers.

"Even if he has my favorite candy, I run."

I had to hold back the chuckle. I thanked my stars every day that Ant is in my life. Kat and I both wanted another child, and we were working on it. I couldn't wait for her stomach to swell with my child.

"That's correct, son. We can work on learning your mom's and my phone number so you can call us immediately."

"You're silly, Daddy. I already know your number and our new address. Those are the first things Mom teaches me when we move."

Ant had suffered through years of running and changing residences, and they must have come up with a routine. I was glad Kat had already taught our son what he needed to know to get hold of us.

"Your mom is smart. We should pick up pizza so she doesn't have to cook."

"Yeah, pizza. Then can I play assassin and bad guy?"

Leave it to Kat to teach our son to play an assassin. We had to work on changing his play habits.

"How about cops and bad guys?" I suggested.

"Okay."

4
KAT

I had seen the tail two miles back. I had tried to get home early so I could do research on Juan before Antonio came home. He didn't want me worried about the case, but I couldn't get Juan and what he had done to my family off my mind. I turned down another street and hoped the car behind me would go the other way, but it turned with me.

"Fuck."

I parked the car in the driveway of our home and watched the car stop a couple houses down. I wasn't born yesterday and knew what the driver had planned, so I worked my way around the side of the house. I wasn't going to let him catch me. There was no way I was going to let someone come into my house and get the drop on me.

The man who came around the corner didn't have

any training. His boots crunched against the rocks on the side of the house. So he wasn't someone Juan had sent after me. No, this guy was just an idiot and didn't know who he was dealing with.

"Who are you?" I yelled as he walked around the corner.

"None of your concern, bitch!" His voice was hoarse from years of smoking.

I took a step to the side and tried to get a good look at his face, but the shadow of the house made it hard to see him clearly. "It is my concern since you followed me. Who sent you?"

"No one sent me. I want you to stay out of my business. You keep putting lies into her head."

"Greg?"

Lily's husband had followed me home. From what I could make out, he was small, maybe five feet six. I had taken down men a lot bigger than him, so it wouldn't be a hard fight if it turned into one. But based on how he treated Lily, I prepared for the worst. At least the dumbass had made my life easier. I didn't have to track him down since he had come to me.

"Yes, you dumb bitch. I came to teach you a lesson about getting into other people's business." He shook his fist at me.

The sun had started to set, and it was taking away what little light I had. We needed to get this settled before I lost my light and Antonio came home. Antonio would make me call the cops and turn him in like a good Samaritan would.

Automatically, I reached for my gun, but it wasn't there. When I went to the women's outreach center, I didn't carry my gun. That would change once I got out of this situation.

"That's funny. Now, tell me what you want before I kill you."

"Tell Lily to come home, and I won't kill you," he yelled back at me.

Lily was safe. Antonio had texted me to say that Jacob had her at one of AA Security's safe houses. Until we took care of Greg, Jacob would be her bodyguard. Antonio knew she meant a great deal to me, and he would do anything to make me happy.

"Yeah, not going to happen. She needs to stay the fuck away from you."

"Don't say I didn't warn you."

I didn't hear the steps behind me until it was too late. My skills weren't as sharp as they normally were, and I'd let my guard down. A body hit me with full force and threw me forward onto the ground. The ground came fast, and I used my hands to brace for impact.

The kick to the rib hurt like a motherfucker. The second kick was on its way. I grabbed my assailant's legs and twisted, which sent the man to the ground with a grunt. I jumped to my feet and side-kicked Greg in the groin. It sent the man to his knees.

Greg wasn't moving for a while. The other man had pulled a gun from his side holster and had it pointed at me. I was used to guns pointed at me. The thug looked over at Greg, who was lying on the ground and crying. I used the opportunity to dodge to the side and pick up a garden gnome Ant had made me buy. I thought the thing was ugly.

I whipped the gnome at the man's head and hit him dead on. I heard the crack of his skull. When I looked to see if Greg was still on the ground, he was gone. There was no sign of him.

I kicked the gun of the unconscious man to the side, then leaned down to check his pulse, but there was none. "Shit."

For the next thirty minutes, when I had planned to do research on Juan, I instead had to hide the dead body I'd created. I had made a promise last week not to kill any more people, but this time, it was an accident. I had meant to knock the man out. Who knew the garden gnome would kill him?

ANTONIO

Kat's car was parked in front of the house, but I couldn't find her anywhere. My heart pounded in fear. Had Juan taken her? Maybe I needed to move us to a safe house and lock her away. She would fight me, but if she were safe, it would be worth it.

"Daddy, someone's in the backyard."

I ran toward the French doors that lead to the backyard. The sight stopped me in my tracks. I told Ant to go play in his room or watch cartoons. He didn't need to see what his mom had done.

I thought I would tan her hide for this one, but it was hard not to chuckle. She was slowly pulling a body across the backyard. It had to be twice her size, and she struggled with each tug. Kat would tug his feet and then take a break. As she pulled the body, the man's head bounced across the rocks in the flower bed. Luckily, our backyard was fenced in, so no one could see her dragging a dead body.

I walked up behind her and wrapped my arms around her waist. She jumped. I held her tighter and whispered in her ear, "Kitty Kat, why are you dragging a dead body across the flower bed?"

"Don't sneak up on me like that. I might have shot you!" She didn't remove herself from my embrace. It felt so good to have her wrapped in my arms, where she belonged. But I had to concentrate on what she had done and not run my hands all over her body. We had to deal with the body on the ground.

"Not an answer. I need to know why there is a body in our yard where I want to put in a pool."

"Umm, I took him out?"

"Clearly. Why?"

She let out an aggravated sigh. "He's friends with Lily's husband."

"Still not a good reason. You said you wanted to get out of the assassin business." I waved my hand at the body. "Seems like you're back in."

"I am out of the assassin business." She pointed at the body. "He followed me home. I told him to leave, or I would kill him."

If I knew my wife, she might have let him leave, but from what I heard had happened to Lily, she hadn't planned on letting Lily's husband live for long. I'd had CJ pull up Lily's police and medical records. She'd had numerous trips to the emergency room for broken bones, and those were just the ones she went in for. How many times had she stayed home and dealt with the damage on her own? I shook my head to get rid of the thoughts.

I had never understood how a man could raise his hand to the woman he loved. I wanted to spend my days worshipping Kat and making sure she had everything she ever wanted.

"Kitty Kat, you need to use your skills to send these men to jail. I know you knew they were following you. You should have called me immediately or called the cops to have them arrested. Promise me there will be no more dead bodies."

Kat bit down on her lip.

"Is there another body back there?"

She stomped her feet in place. "No, he got away. Lily's husband, Greg, escaped. I didn't mean to kill this guy, but when I threw the garden gnome at his head… well, this is what happened."

I couldn't hold in my laughter. My five-foot-three Kitty Kat had killed an overgrown thug with a garden gnome. At least she hadn't hunted this guy down herself. She was attacked at our house, which lead me back to the idea of sending her to a safe house. Maybe Zane would side with me, and we could send Sophie along for company. That way they wouldn't argue about it if they were together.

"No!" she yelled.

I crossed my arms over my chest. "You don't even know what I was going to say."

Kat went back to tugging the body across the yard. With each tug at the man's feet, she grunted, using all her strength to move him. The sun had gone down, and the porch light was the only light in the backyard.

She dropped the feet of the dead body and gave me

her full attention. "You were plotting a way to get me into a safe house. Not gonna happen." When I opened my mouth, she cut me off. "Even if you put Sophie in there with me. We'll escape and go after not only Juan but you as well for putting us in there."

One thing about our relationship was that we could read each other, and she guessed my thoughts. I let it go for the moment, but the thought of losing my wife again left an ugly taste in my mouth.

"Fine. No safe house." Her face lit with joy. "As long as you don't remove the trackers and you stop killing people."

"Bu—"

I cut her off. "Did you have your phone on you?"

Kat reached down, grabbed the body, and continued to drag it. I knew I should help her, but it was cute seeing her try to move it.

"Answer the question."

She dropped the feet again and put her hands on her hips. Her red hair was hanging down in her face. "Yes!"

I grabbed her and brought her into my arms. "No safe house as long as you call the cops next time you are being followed. No more taking on the bad guy. Now, you want to explain what you had planned to do with the body?"

For some reason, I was worried about her answer.

She knew exactly where she was heading. I didn't want to know what was at the end of the trail.

She rubbed her body against mine, trying to distract me. I didn't think she would answer me at first, but she said, "I found that if I can get a dead body in the storm drain over there"—she pointed to the back of the property, toward a gate that led to a retention pond for collecting the runoff from the neighboring lots—"the alligators come and eat them. They wait for the bodies I bring them."

As if shocked at herself, she reached up and put a hand over her mouth, but a hand over her mouth didn't take the words back.

"Kitty Kat, how many bodies have you dumped down there?"

She winced. "How many is too many?"

How to answer? A normal person would have said one. But knowing my wife, it was more than one already. I took a few calming breaths before giving my answer.

"Five. Five is way too many."

"Okay. Less than five."

Her words came out way too quickly. I figured she had fed the alligators more than five bodies. We would never get rid of them. The only option was to move, because the alligators sure as hell would never leave us alone if she kept them fed.

"It's more, isn't it?"

"Maybe."

I tried to pry her away from my body so I could see her eyes. "You want to tell me who you've been killing? I thought you said you only killed this man because he followed you home."

"That's why I killed *him*." She pointed to the man lying at our feet.

I gritted my teeth and held back what I wanted to say. "Tell me about the others."

"Fine. One of the girls at the shelter was brutally raped many times by a gang. She escaped to the facility and has been in hiding. She's scared to be touched. The story she told me broke my heart."

Kat had no sense of how dangerous her actions were. Taking on a gang of men was too much. She had a family to think about. She needed to rely on me and stop taking on the world by herself.

"You tracked these people down and took them out alone? When did you find time to do that?"

"I had help finding out about their motorcycle bar and routine. They left the bar every day at noon. I set up my sniper rifle and took them out on my lunch break. I have to tell you, I love the size of the Navigator we got."

"You can't spend your lunch break killing people. You are no longer an assassin!" I paced back and forth, trying to deal with my anger. "I didn't buy you a big SUV so you could haul around dead bodies. The SUV is supposed to be large and safe."

I heard Ant running toward our location in the backyard, and a groan escaped my throat. I didn't have time to scoop him up before he saw the body lying at our feet.

"Mommy, is that a dead body?" Ant picked up a stick and poked the body. Our son would probably have nightmares. I knew I sure as hell would. My wife had taken out a biker gang on her lunch break, for heaven's sake.

I reached down and pulled Ant into my arms then moved so he couldn't see the body any longer. "You were supposed to be watching cartoons."

"I saw you and Mommy in the backyard, and I wanted to play."

I leaned over and kissed Kat on the forehead before passing our son over to her. "How about you take our son back inside while I take care of this?"

"Thank you for helping."

"I will always be there for you, Kitty Kat. But this?" I pointed to the dead body. "You need to stop."

Kat was heading toward the porch when she replied over her shoulder. "Next time I have an issue, I will call you before taking care of it myself. But if I don't have a choice, I will take out the enemy."

"Go inside," I growled.

Once she and Ant had disappeared into the house, I reached for my phone and dialed Zane. He would give me shit about this for a long time, but Kat's plan to feed the body to the alligators wouldn't be an option.

The phone rang a couple times before he answered. Without a greeting, I got straight to the point. "Zane, do you know a good cleanup crew around here?"

"Is everyone okay?"

"Yes. My wife doesn't like how the women at the shelter have been treated. She took someone out. Two of them followed her home, and instead of calling the cops, she led them into a trap and took one of them out."

The laughter that exploded through the phone didn't ease the headache I was experiencing because of my wife's habits. She had spent her childhood learning how to take people out, and her adulthood was no different. I knew it would take time for her to adjust. I just didn't expect the body count to be more than six in a month.

"Stop. Laughing. I have a dead body I need to get rid of."

"Someone will be there within the hour." He barely got the words out because he was still laughing so loud.

But I knew how to get back at him. Kat hadn't done all the research on her own. She'd had help.

"Who do you think helped my wife with the other five bodies she put in the drainage tunnel, Zane? She fucking fed the dead bodies to alligators! How am I going to get rid of alligators when she keeps feeding them?"

The laughter stopped quickly when he figured out his fiancée had put herself in harm's way. "I'll have a talk with Soph."

Feeling vindicated, I clicked the phone off and dragged the dead body to the side of the house. The cleanup crew would deal with it. I wanted to spend the night with my wife and kid.

From the porch, I could see Ant and Kat at the table, and I couldn't believe how lucky I was to have them back in my life. Even if my wife liked to kill people.

/ 5

KAT

I took another bite of the Hawaiian pizza. The conversation around the table felt so normal. It didn't feel like Ant and I had been away from Antonio for years.

The sound of car doors being slammed had me reaching for the gun I no longer carried. Tomorrow, I would start carrying again. I had little doubt Greg would come for me a second time. Greg wanted his wife, and I stood between him and the woman he wanted.

When Antonio didn't move to see who was at the front, I stood up from the espresso wood chair.

"Sit, Kitty Kat."

"I'm going to see who's here." He had to have heard the car door slam and the men's voices in our yard.

Antonio reached over and ruffled Ant's hair before he answered. "It's a cleanup crew."

The poor alligators weren't going to get a feast. They enjoyed the treats I had brought them. It wasn't fair to cut off their food supply.

Ant looked up at his dad. "Daddy, what's a cleanup crew?"

My dear husband leveled a glare in my direction. He didn't want to tell our son that the body in the backyard that had lain in the purple tulips was a dead body and not a man that fell asleep. A wheelbarrow would be a nice addition to the garden supplies. If I could get the dead body in a wheelbarrow, I wouldn't leave drag marks across the backyard and destroy the pretty flowers the housekeeper Judy had planted.

It had taken time to get used to a housekeeper. Judy was in her late fifties and had worked for Antonio for ten years. She cleaned the house and prepared meals for us to pull out of the fridge and cook during the week. Ant adored her, mostly because she baked him fresh cookies.

Life in Antonio's house had taken me a while to get used to. Ant and I had moved from apartment to apartment. My old job had required me to be on the move, so we never stayed in the same place very long.

"They are here to clean up the back flower gardens."

Ant pondered my answer for a second before he responded. "You mean the dead guy?"

Across the table, Antonio spit out his sip of beer. "That man was asleep. There was no dead body in the backyard." His deep, rich voice carried through the dining room.

If I hadn't killed the guy with my own hands, I might've believed the words that came out of Antonio's mouth. Over the years, I hadn't always had a sitter to take care of Ant. He'd seen more than anyone his age should. He also knew we weren't supposed to talk about the dead bodies.

"Daddy, you're silly. I saw Mommy pulling the body. She was going to feed our pet alligator."

I loved my son to death, but he was getting me in trouble. Antonio let out a sigh and gave me a look that had me squirming in my seat. The conversation wasn't over. I could tell by his look that Antonio planned to talk about it later, in private.

It was hard to hold back the laugh. I slid out of my chair, hoping to get out of the room before either of them said another word. I made it two steps across the white marble floor before Antonio told me to sit. The thought that I should ignore him crossed my mind.

"Son..." Antonio began. He looked up at the ceiling and pinched the bridge of his nose. "What you sa—"

"It's okay, Dad. I know not to talk about it to anyone other than Mom. Mom says she's going to quit killing bad men." His little lip trembled. "But then who will feed the alligators? Will they starve?"

"No, buddy. They will eat other animals." I said.

"Okay." He seemed satisfied with my answer. "Can I go play with my army men now?"

I nodded, and he leaped out of his booster seat and sprinted down the hall. I didn't have time to tell him to slow down before he was gone. I grabbed the plates off the table to clean up the dinner mess.

"Leave it, Kitty Kat. Come here."

I expected to see disappointment in my husband's eyes. Instead, his pupils dilated, and he shifted in his seat. When I was within arm's reach, he pulled me down onto his lap. His erection pressed against me. I shifted in his lap and rubbed against his length.

"Stop," he growled. "What am I going to do with you?"

"Love me the way I am." I leaned in and brushed my lips across his. They tasted of beer.

"I can't help but be turned on by you taking that man out. But we can't have our son seeing things like that." The hint of disappointment in his voice was enough for me to stop being selfish. I needed to make the right decisions according to the law, not according to what I wanted. He was right—our son should not have seen the dead body in the backyard or have known I'd fed bodies to the alligators.

"I promise I will ask for help. No more killing." Well, unless it was Juan. Antonio didn't need to know I still planned on taking my uncle out.

I had straddled Antonio in the dining room chair. He used his two large hands to cup my ass and stand. It took me by surprise, and I let out a loud squeal.

Antonio carried me back to our room. His muscular arms flexed with each step he took. A tattoo of an eagle peaked out from the bottom of his black T-shirt. He was the most handsome man I had ever laid eyes on, and most days, I couldn't believe he was mine.

He glanced in Ant's room on the way by. Ant had his army and cop figurines spread across the floor. He wouldn't bother us until it was time for bed. Just in case, we would lock the door to make sure our little man saw nothing that would scare him.

I could feel Antonio's heartbeat against my rib cage. He was as excited as I was to get naked. The adrenaline from earlier still ran through my veins. I couldn't wait to see Antonio strip out of his clothes and run my hands along his six-pack.

When we entered our room, he sat me on the bed, locked the door, and turned on Ant's one-way speaker so we could hear if he needed us.

He pulled me back up and touched his lips to mine. Every time he pulled me in for a kiss, my legs went weak and the world faded away. His tongue swiped across my mouth and demanded entrance. He caressed my cheek with his thumb as we devoured each other.

I was lost in the kiss when Antonio pulled back. I groaned at the loss of his touch. My body wanted me to climb Antonio and demand he hurry up. We had time for romance later. I needed to feel Antonio inside me.

"I want you now."

Antonio grinned down at me. "I want to go slow and kiss every inch of your body."

I let out a frustrated sigh. "We can go slow later."

He laid me down on the bed. "Kitty Kat, you need to learn patience." After a beat, he asked, "Are you comfortable?"

"Yes," I grumbled. There was no point in arguing with him.

"Good, because I have you right where I want you."

"But I want to ride you. Can we do missionary later?"

Antonio leaned down, nipped my ear, and whispered, "I'm in charge right now. Lie back and feel." He licked the soft skin behind my ear, causing a tingle to course through my body. Antonio's tongue was pure magic and lit my body on fire. It was hard to hold my composure when he whispered in my ear. Each day my body yearned for him more.

The words caught in my mouth as Antonio slid his hands under my shirt and cupped my full breasts. When Antonio lifted his gaze, I could see his eyes were heavy with lust and need. When he lifted my shirt over my head, he didn't break eye contact.

After I had come in from outside earlier, I'd showered and hadn't put a bra back on. Antonio groaned when he took my shirt off and my boobs were displayed. He lowered his head to my breasts and wrapped his warm mouth around one nipple. He used his free hand to cup my other breast.

"Antonio, please."

I shifted under him, trying to push my pelvis up for friction. "More. I need more." His touch left my body in flames.

"More of this?" he asked before pinching my other nipple. He released my nipple and gazed up at me. A ruthless smile spread across his face. He knew what his touch did to me.

"Touch me."

"You want me to touch you here?"

"Antonio..." His name was almost inaudible as he reached his hand down my yoga pants.

"Nothing better than hearing you say my name. You're all worked up, Kitty Kat, and I haven't put my lips on this pretty pussy yet."

It took everything in me not to yell out in frustration. Antonio sat up, and at the loss of the connection, I whined. He reached down and pulled his T-shirt over his body. His abs flexed with the movement. I yearned to run my tongue over his golden-brown skin. The three bullet-wound scars on his chest brought a moment of sadness. It was a reminder of the time we had lost.

Antonio crawled back onto the bed and worked my yoga pants down my legs. His hands skimmed over my skin, and it caused my body to ignite. When my pants were off and on the floor, Antonio threw each of my legs over his shoulders. Before he settled between my knees, he gave the tattoo on my hip a kiss. It was the name "Antonio" written inside a heart.

"Now, this is dessert," Antonio whispered before he took my clit in his mouth.

I hadn't had time to register his words before my body went on alert for his tongue. My legs were spread wide to accommodate his broad shoulders, and he put his hands under my butt and lifted so he had full access.

"Oh, my god... yeah." Antonio had gone from slowly lapping at my clit to full gusto. I gripped his arms and tried to cause more friction. He slapped my leg with his hand, sending an extra wave of arousal through my body.

"You will take what I give you."

"More..." I whined.

"More what?"

I didn't have time to respond before he pulled his mouth from my clit and slid his two fingers into me. God, I was in heaven. When he saw I was close to the edge, he leaned back down and flicked his tongue hard and fast. The slight scruff on his face sent another sensation through me.

"Right there. Shit... yeah... I can't hold back!"

My body arched when I went over the edge. Antonio continued his relentless pressure on my clit and continued to pump his two fingers in and out. I rode his fingers until the last wave of my orgasm faded. Then Antonio pulled his fingers from my folds and licked them clean.

I could feel my juices running down my leg. Even though I had come a second ago, I wanted my legs wrapped around Antonio's body. I tugged at his arms to come up. "I need you inside me. Please, Antonio."

Antonio climbed up my body and whispered, "Put me where you want me." I reached between us and grabbed Antonio's hard member. Antonio moved his hips and pushed in. We'd had a lot of sex since we reconnected, but every time, I felt so full when he thrust into me.

Our eyes connected, and the love that shone in his was so strong that I almost had to look away. "I love you," I whispered. Antonio pulled back and thrust in hard, then he leaned down and brushed his lips against mine. "I love you too, Kitty Kat."

I gripped Antonio's shoulders and tried to get him to move faster. My body was close to going over the edge a second time. He hit my G-spot with each thrust. Antonio reached his hand between us and pinched my clit, which caused me to come for the second time.

My velvety folds clenched against his member. Antonio followed me over, thrusting deep inside me one last time.

After a moment, Antonio leaned down and took my lips before rolling me to the side and pulling me tight against his body.

"You were amazing, love," Antonio whispered.

"You did all the work."

Antonio ran his hand up and down my arm, and it sent shivers through my body. "God, I'm happy I have you back in my life."

Not much later, I realized I had fallen asleep in his arms. He moved to get up, and I went to get up with him. But he leaned down and said, "Sleep, Kat, I'm going to go put our son to bed."

6

ANTONIO

The following morning at the office was filled with paperwork. I missed the days when I got to spend time out in the field and not behind the desk. The reports that needed to be read were piled up, and I needed to figure out which case we would take next. Jacob's report regarding Lily was in my hand when my office door swung open.

Asher came in and sat in the leather chair in front of my desk. Zane followed behind and folded his large body into the other chair. The smiles plastered across their faces told me why they were in my office.

"I heard you caught your wife trying to hide a dead body."

"Do you guys do any work, or do you sit around and gossip like women?"

"It's not every day you find out your sister-in-law hasn't given up her side job as an assassin."

I glanced at the picture on my desk. Kat sat on the back patio, her red hair pulled up into a bun. She wore a tight white shirt that accented her curves. Ant sat on her lap, and they had smiles across their faces. My kitty cat of a wife might be small, but she was lethal.

"She's done." I pointed at Zane. "You need to make sure Sophie stops helping her."

Zane leaned back in the chair. "You're under the impression we can stop Kat and Sophie from doing what they want. Even though they have been separated from each other for years, I can tell they are sisters. Those two have been on their own for most of their lives, and they think they have to take on the world by themselves."

"Goddammit, she *will* listen."

"I doubt it. But we don't have time to argue about that. Yesterday, Asher and I went through the list of names John sent us. One of the names on the list was Nebula Brack. CJ looked into the guy more and discovered he was a radical hiding under the guise of a doomsday prepper. His arrest list is a mile long—domestic violence, assault with a deadly weapon, and failure to pay taxes. He used his cover as a prepper to store guns in his underground bunker."

Nebula had been our only lead, and it was a dead

end. We needed a break in the case. Juan needed to be taken out.

"I take it he's dead?"

Zane tossed the folder in his hand on the desk. When I opened the folder, it was filled with pictures of an underground bunker and a dead man.

"We infiltrated his bunker. He's been dead for at least twenty-four hours. I bet Sanchez was waiting for him when he returned. The place had been turned upside down. Someone was looking for something, but we're not sure they found what they were looking for."

Asher leaned forward to point at the man in the photo. "Whoever killed him, besides turning the place upside down, cleaned out the weapon room of the bunker. From the cases that were left, we're guessing they took heavy-grade military weapons. We need to let the FBI know."

If we did, the FBI would want to take over the case. There were parts of the case that weren't top secret. Director Charles Westblack had been a longtime friend of our family. He would be angry with me when he found out I left him in the dark. But he would want to take over the case. If it were any other case, I would call it in. This one was ours to solve and Juan ours to take down.

Before I could voice my thoughts, Zane said, "We can alert Charles once Sanchez is dead. I don't want any Feds butting their noses into this case. If we find something for the FBI, I will send Charles a report when we are done." Zane had as much at stake as I did—probably a little more because of his brother.

I glanced down at the file. Things weren't adding up. "Why kill the bomb guy before you know you have completed a mission? Or was he watching from the bunker and took him out because he was angry the mission failed? Doomsday people like that have cameras everywhere. Did you find any video footage?" I asked.

Asher flipped to a picture of the bunker's command area. "Someone took a hammer to the camera's DVR server. CJ is working on recovering data from the disc. He's pretty sure he will have it by the end of the day."

"Call me as soon as the video footage comes in. I'm having lunch with Kat. Zane, can you look at the Limburger case?"

Mr. Limburger's daughter had been missing for close to a year, and the trail the police had found went dry. Mr. Limburger was a friend of my father's and asked if AA Security could take a look at the case.

Zane nodded before he stood up from the chair. Before he exited the door to my office, he turned to tell me one last thing. "Make sure your wife doesn't murder anyone."

"Fuck off."

Once Zane and Asher exited my office, I went back to reading the file about Lily. Jacob reported that she had multiple bruises. Her husband had tried to come after her while they were exiting the testing center the previous day. Jacob apprehend him and called the police. Kat couldn't kill him if he was in jail. One less item on my plate.

"GODDAMMIT."

I wanted to have a quick lunch with my wife. Instead, when I came to the parking lot at the Women's Center, I found Kat's SUV with "Bitch" painted across the side. I needed to figure out if Juan did it or if Greg had gotten out of jail.

I reached into my pocket to grab my phone and selected Kat from the favorites. "Kat, I'm going to have to cancel our lunch."

If I told her about the car, she would want to come out and see what was going on. I needed her to stay inside until I figured out who we were dealing with. I took a couple more steps toward the SUV and noticed the front tire was slashed.

"Okay. I'll run to the deli and grab something." Kat's words tore my attention away from the SUV.

"No!" I yelled.

"Oh, when have I ever listened to you? I'm hungry. It will only take a second." Kat didn't wait for my answer. She clicked off the phone.

I didn't have time to call her back. My phone rang again immediately, and Neal's name flashed across the screen. Neal was the CEO of Black Hat Security. He was an excellent hacker, and when our caseload got too large, he helped us out. CJ's plate was full with the Juan case and the video he needed to retrieve. I needed someone to retrieve the video footage from around the Women's Center.

I swiped across the phone to answer. "Hey, Neal. I was about to call you."

"I was calling to see if you were joining us for poker night tomorrow?"

"Sure. What time?"

"Club Sanctorum at nine. Now, what can I help you with?"

Once a month, Brock closed Club Sanctorum for poker night. Club Sanctorum wasn't the only thing in the building. Blackwood Security was on the second floor, and the top floor held three apartments. The place also had top-of-the-line security. I felt safe taking Kat there. She could meet up with the girls while we played poker.

"Could you pull up the security cameras near Ross Women's Outreach Center?"

"Give me a second." I could hear his fingers fly across the keyboard. "I can see you. What do you want me to look for?" Neal was as good as CJ, probably even better, but I wouldn't tell my brother-in-law that. I would end up electronically dead or on the no-fly list.

"I'm standing next to Kat's car, and it's been vandalized. Could you look through the video from this morning and see if you can find out who did it? I'm going to call the police and file a report."

"No problem. I will call when I have something."

"Thanks. I owe you one. We're short-staffed right now. Everyone is working on Juan's case, and I'm hesitant to bring in more people from White Hat."

Sophie worked at White Hat, and she would want to work on the Juan case. Anything she would find she would take to her sister or keep from me. I knew Kat and her sister wanted to be the ones to take Juan out. I didn't blame them. But I didn't want my wife or sister-in-law to get hurt.

"Why? You worried your wife will find out and kill them?" Neal laughed through the phone.

"How have you already heard about this?"

"It was announced in a group text."

The friends in our inner circle needed to have more activities in their lives. Kat's killing people was the least of my worries. I was worried we didn't know exactly who was after her this time.

"Call me with what you find, and stop encouraging my wife's killing habit."

I was examining the tire when I heard the click of high heels. I knew who it was before I saw her. I wish she would have listened to me. Whoever vandalized her car could be watching.

I pulled her into my arms before she got too close to the car. "I thought I told you to stay in."

"Why are you here, and why didn't you want to have lunch?" She peeked around my shoulder and looked at her car. "I'm going to fucking kill him!"

She tried to pull out of my arms. I tightened my hold around her waist. "You know who did this?"

Kat rested her head on my chest, giving into my need to have her in my arms. "Well, no, but I will kill the person when I find out who it is."

This was the reason I didn't want her to see what happened. She didn't think to call the police. She went straight to the need to kill the person who vandalized her car. "You promised no more killing. I called the cops, and here they come." I pointed in the direction of the cop car. "You call the cops when there is an issue. You don't take care of it yourself."

Kat pulled away from my arms. She rested her hands on her hips, giving me her full attention. "I highly doubt every time you find something the cops should know about, you send them your report."

I ignored her statement and greeted the detective that walked our way. "Detective Higgins, I would like you to meet my wife, Katherine Ross." Higgins reached out his hand and greeted us both.

Detective Higgins had been with the local police force for thirty years. Over the past few years, we had worked a few cases with him. He was in his fifties and one of the hardest-working detectives I knew. Higgins would work overtime to make sure the bad guy went to jail.

"Nice to meet you, Mrs. Ross. What can I do for you?"

I motioned for him to walk with me toward Kat's SUV. "I came to meet Kat for lunch, and I found her car like this."

Detective Higgins bent down to look at the tire and took pictures of the tire and the side of the car. "This looks like it was done in anger. Can you think of anyone you might have upset?"

"A few people."

"How can such a lovely lady have a few people after her?"

I knew Higgins was joking with my wife, but his flirtations made me see red. I wanted to punch him in the face. "Stop flirting with my wife. We need to figure out who is after her."

Higgins wrote the details in his notebook and put it in his front pocket. "Always a man straight to the point. Never any fun." He pointed in my direction and winked at my wife. "If you ever get sick of Antonio, call me."

"We don't need your help," I grumbled.

"I like getting a rise out of you."

My phone vibrated with a text from Neal letting me know what he found on the cameras near the Women's Center.

"A friend of mine pulled video footage of the perp. Video quality sucks, though. All he could see was a man in a hooded black sweater and a black cap, white, about five feet eight. Sprayed the car and went down the alley. You want me to send the video to you?"

Higgins looked like he would take me up on the offer at first. Then he sighed. "No, I will find the video the proper way. Your guy probably hacked some cameras. We'll see if we can get video from the alley. In the meantime, stay safe, and let us handle the case." Higgins didn't wait for us to respond before heading back to his car.

"Will do, Detective," Kat called after him.

The twinkle in her eye told me she had other plans, and she wouldn't call the cops if something like this happened again. I wouldn't be surprised if she asked Sophie to pull the video footage when I looked at my phone to respond to Neal.

"Why don't I believe a word that came out of your mouth?"

Since she had already seen what I had tried to hide, I whisked Kat away for lunch.

7
KAT

Antonio, his brothers, Zane, Brock, and a few men I didn't know were downstairs at the poker table set up in Club Sanctorum. Earlier, Antonio and I had walked through the club before heading up to Brock and Jessica's apartment on the third floor. The club had been transformed for the night. In place of the spanking bench was the poker table. All the other BDSM equipment had been packed away.

The laughter in Brock and Jessica's kitchen brought a smile to my face. Over the past few weeks, Bridget and Jessica had brought me into their fold. Being an assassin, I never had time to stop and make friends, and I hated to lie about what I did for a living.

I still hadn't met Patty or Sam. Patty was Jessica's twin sister and the future queen of Shialia. Her future husband used to own Club Sanctorum and Blackwood

Security. When Patty had to take over for her father, who had disappeared, Patty and Sam gave everything to Brock. We were supposed to be headed to Shialia for their wedding in the next few weeks. But something had happened in Shialia, and the wedding was put on hold.

Jessica and Sophie sat at the island and snacked on a cheese tray.

"Red or white?" Bridget held a wine bottle in each hand. Each bottle had the Ross family's name and crest on the label. My husband's family had mastered every market I could think of. It was hard to fathom how much his family was worth. I was still dealing with the fact that I was worth a billion dollars from my own trust.

I pointed to her right hand, which held the bottle of white wine. "Fill it to the top. It's been a long day." I enjoyed my days at the women's center, but it was hard to see what these women went through. I wanted to help everyone that walked through the doors. Earlier, a woman I had never seen before showed up with her three-year-old boy. Both the mother and son had black and blue marks on their bodies. It took everything in me not to head out the door and find the man who hurt them.

My afternoon had been spent checking her into the facility, and I made sure she and her son had everything they needed. The fact she had taken steps to get out of harm's way made me feel better.

"Is not being able to kill someone wearing on your soul? I figured you and Antonio would be making up for years of no sex. How do you have time to kill people?"

Leave it to Bridget to get straight to the point without giving me time to have a couple glasses of wine. They had included me in the group text that talked about my habit of killing people. I chose to ignore the text messages. It was harder to ignore people who stood in front of you.

"I killed five people, and everyone has an issue."

Sophie grabbed a piece of cheese from the tray before asking, "Only five?"

"Fine. A few more than five. Does it really matter how many? If you would have seen what happened to these women at the shelter, every one of you would've done the same. Lily came into the shelter last week with a limp and a black-and-blue eye. When her husband and his friend came after me for keeping him from Lily, I had no qualms about defending myself. I would've preferred to kill Greg, though, rather than the man he brought along."

"Speaking of women needing help to protect themselves, when are you going to do another self-defense class? Tomorrow would be great. Your classes always help me relieve stress. Mr. Ross has been extra cranky at work, and it is driving me crazy."

Tomorrow was my first day off from the women's center. I had worked at the center nonstop for the past two weeks, and I wanted to spend my day off on some leads I had on Juan.

Bridget set down her apple juice. She kept Sophie's and my wine glasses flowing with wine, but Jessica and Bridget were both drinking apple juice. "Don't let my husband push you around. He's under stress about the second baby." She rubbed her hand across the bulge of her six-month belly. "Tomorrow would work great for me too. I need to get in as many classes as possible before I can't see my toes again."

"Tomorrow is not going to work for me," I said.

"Why not?" Sophie asked. She leveled her eyes at me and waited for the excuse I was going to make up.

I spouted the first thing that came to mind. "I'm working at the shelter."

"Liar. I know you aren't working at the shelter. Try again." I loved having Sophie back in my life, but it made it harder to get away with undercover work.

"I'm volunteering at Ant's school."

Sophie shook her head, not buying my excuse.

"Grocery shopping?"

"Try again."

"Going to the mall?"

"You buy everything on Amazon. Do you even know where a mall is?"

She was right. If I ran out of anything, I bought it on Amazon. When I arrived home each night, it was like Christmas. Half of the time, I didn't know what was in the box I was about to open. Sophie would keep on me until I told her what I was planning, or she would show up at my house tomorrow and follow me.

"Fine. I found out Antonio is keeping information from me about the Sanchez case. I'm going to go check out the information."

"Why are you sure he is keeping anything from you?" Jessica asked.

I really didn't want to admit that I had bugged my husband and listened to his conversations at work. I did it because he kept information on the case from me. I trusted him with everything else. My heart belonged to him and his to me. But he would do anything to keep me safe, and that included not telling me what information he'd found.

"I overheard him." I reached for the bottle of wine to refill my glass, more for something to do than because I wanted more. If I looked at Sophie, she would see right through me.

"Then why don't you confront him about it?"

"Hmm." I took a big gulp of the wine. "We might not have been in the same place."

"How did you hear the conversation if you weren't in the same place?"

"I had a feeling information was being withheld. There is a chance I put a bug in his suit jacket this morning."

Sophie jumped from her seat. She had been the last to get attacked by Juan when he put a bomb in her car. Knowing Zane hadn't told her something had her face turning red. "Tell me what they said. I have a right to know," Sophie demanded.

In the past, I had done all my jobs alone. It was hard to involve the people around me, especially when I didn't want any of them to get hurt. I knew my sister would find the information one way or another, so as I reached for the glass of wine, I said, "Antonio found the person who put the bomb in your car. Zane went to the bun—"

"My fiancé knows who put the bomb in my car?" Sophie's eyes narrowed.

Fuck. Antonio would be pissed about my plan, and now I'd also made my sister mad at Zane. If she went off on him, he would ask how she found out, and my plan would be ruined.

Bridget spoke up before I had time to explain. "Hold on a second. Let's head to the living room and get comfy. I want to hear what you have planned."

Bridget didn't wait for any of our replies. She

grabbed her apple juice and a platter of food and headed toward the living room.

Once seated, I grabbed a pink throw pillow from the couch and pulled it to my chest. "Sophie, you can't let Zane know you found out about the bomber." When her eyes narrowed in my direction, I continued. "Then you will have to tell him how you figured it out. I plan on going to the bunker tomorrow morning. After I get all the information I need, you can scream at him all you want."

Sophie didn't reply right away. When we were younger, she would analyze all her options before she would agree to anything. Her far-off look was an indicator she didn't want to wait to talk to Zane and was trying to come up with a way around it, but it seemed she couldn't.

"Fine, but the second we get the information, I'm chewing his ass out. I have a right to know who put that bomb in my car. Zane thinks he's protecting me by not telling me, but it only makes me madder when he keeps important information from me."

"We need to come up with a plan for tomorrow," Bridget added.

"A plan? Whatever it is, you can't come, Bridget. I love you, but no way am I putting you or your baby in danger."

Bridget let out a huff. "Of course, I'm not going. I

might like to help, but I draw the line at putting my baby in danger." She pointed at Sophie. "You and Sophie are going tomorrow because I don't want either of you going alone. You will both go where there are webcams connected to White Hat Security so Jessica and I can watch."

The mission to see what I could dig up at the bunker would be dangerous. Sophie worked behind a computer. I didn't want her to come in the field with me. The thought that she might get shot or hurt sent my stomach into a tumble. "Sophie can stay with you at White Hat. I will wear the camera and a com.

Sophie leaned back in the couch and folded her arms. "Do you ever see Antonio send his men into the field by themselves?"

"No, but I'm a trained assassin and have worked alone for years."

"So you're saying Antonio's men aren't trained as well as you?"

There was no way to win this argument. Antonio had some of the best men and women I had ever met. He hired ex-military who were the best of the best, but they worked better as a team. In the years I'd worked for the CIA, I worked alone. It was hard to change and take help from others, especially when I was concerned they would get hurt.

I let out a sigh of defeat. "No, I'm not better than Antonio's men. I just don't want any of you to get hurt.

"But it's okay for us to let you get hurt?" Bridget asked.

"Fine. If it makes everyone happy, Sophie can come with me."

Suddenly, the door to Jessica and Brock's apartment flew open. In the doorway stood CJ, Asher's partner and Bridget's best friend.

CJ strode in and engulfed Bridget in a hug before taking a seat in the black recliner. I still didn't know where CJ's loyalties lay. I knew he planned to work for Asher and Antonio. Would he tell them my plan, or would he stay on our side?

Leaning back in the chair, CJ asked, "What's the latest gossip?"

Before I had time to say anything, Bridget chimed in. "Kat's bugged Antonio, and she knows he's kept things from her. She and Sophie are going to go check out a bunker."

CJ's faced paled at Bridget's words. I wasn't sure if he was worried I might get hurt or if he thought I told Bridget about him being hired at AA Security.

"You heard all his conversations today?" CJ croaked out.

Bridget gave CJ a puzzled look. "Of course she did. Didn't you just hear what I told you?"

He nodded and cracked the beer in his hand. He took a couple big gulps. I knew he was worried about what was said. I needed to put his worries aside. It wasn't my place to tell Sophie and Bridget he had taken another job.

"I told them everything Antonio talked about with regards to Juan."

CJ nodded at me. He understood I hadn't let his secret out of the bag. He would have to tell her soon, or she would figure it out on her own.

Conversation about how we would run the op flowed for the next hour. Once Antonio left for the office and I dropped Ant off at school, I would head over to White Hat Security. Bridget had a camera and ear coms I would wear that would link back to her servers and record everything I see or hear. That way, everything we saw or heard would be recorded.

We could come back and analyze the video afterward to see if there was anything we missed.

I looked down at my watch and noticed it was late. We needed to stop by Antonio's parents' house and pick up Ant. He loved to spend time with his grandparents, but I still had a hard time being away from him for too long.

"I think it's time for me to head out."

I said my goodbyes to the women in the room. We

all confirmed the time we were meeting tomorrow. CJ was the last to walk up and give me a hug goodbye.

"Thank you," he whispered in my ear.

If I could hold his secret, he needed to hold mine. "Please don't tell the guys what I'm planning."

I felt his body stiffen under my arms, but he agreed. He wasn't happy about it, but I wasn't happy keeping information from my sister and Bridget, either.

As we pulled apart, the door to the apartment swung open. Antonio stood in the doorway with a scowl across his face.

"Why do you have your hands on my wife?"

I walked over and wrapped my arms around Antonio's waist. "Stop, hun. We were saying goodbye. He's going to be my brother in-law, you can't get jealous of your gay future brother inlaw."

"I still think a goodbye handshake is better," he grumbled as he led me out the door.

The next day would be an eventful one. I tossed and turned all night, unable to sleep. I felt slightly remorseful about the secret I was keeping from Antonio.

8

KAT

I gripped the steering wheel and glanced at my surroundings. A small fishing cabin sat in the middle of the property. I reached over to the passenger side and grabbed the piece of paper with the coordinates. I was in the correct location. I took a couple of deep breaths and stepped out of the rented SUV.

The gravel cracked underneath the soles of my combat boots. I reached to my side and checked for my Glock. I was rewarded with the feel of my gun. It made me feel safer for a moment.

I had promised Bridget and Sophie that I wouldn't come to Nebula's bunker. Zane had been called to Washington by his brother, and Sophie went with him. We planned to go to the bunker together when she returned on Friday. I was all for the plan to wait until she returned. But when I left White Hat Security earlier, I started to drive, and a half hour later, I ended up at the location I swore I wouldn't go to alone.

The air in Florida was hot and sticky. I wasn't used to it. Ant and I had spent most of our time in the northeast corner of the country. Every time I stepped into the Florida sun, I felt like I needed to take a shower.

My phone vibrated in my pocket, and it made me jump in surprise. I pulled out my phone to see who was calling. When Sophie's name flashed across the screen, my stomach turned with remorse. I ignored her call and put the phone in my pocket. Not two seconds later, the phone rang again. By the fourth time she called, I knew she wouldn't stop.

"Hey, sis." I leaned against the rental and took in the surroundings.

I heard her huff on the other end of the line. "Don't 'hey' me. What have you found?"

I looked down the abandoned road to make sure I wasn't followed. "I don't know what you are talking about." I couldn't see anyone for miles.

"Bullshit! I don't have much time to talk. Zane is talking to Antonio. Have you found anything?"

"I just got here." There was no point in lying. She would pester me until I told her the truth. I walked toward the abandoned building. The Florida sun beat down with no remorse. I had been out of the car for two minutes and already felt the sweat drip down my back.

"Damn, I'm good. I knew you wouldn't be able to wait. Hell, I would've done the same."

The thought of Sophie going rogue sent a shiver down my back. Sophie was excellent at the computer stuff that I didn't understand or care to learn. But she wasn't skilled in the field.

"Please tell me that if you find anything on Juan, you won't go alone." If I lost her again, it would crush me.

"I'm not stupid, Kat. Now, tell me what you see."

There was a trail that led from the fishing cabin toward the back of the property. "I'm following a trail. I think it will lead either to the underground bunker or into a swamp of alligators."

I almost missed the shine of the metal door on the ground. It had been covered with grass to obscure the location. I reached for my gun.

"Zane's coming back, so I need to let you go. Text me what you find. Be safe, Kat. I just got you back. I don't want to lose you again.

"Call me later, and I will tell you everything I find."

I brushed the grass and weeds off the manhole cover. I set my gun beside me, reached for the two handles on each side of the door, and pulled with all my weight. It opened slowly. The door was heavy, and it took all my strength to pry it open. It thudded against the ground when it fell on the other side of the hinge. I wasn't sure I would be able to close the door again.

I glanced around to make sure no one had followed me to the middle of nowhere, then readied my Glock. The hole I had opened was dark and daunting. I took a deep breath and worked my way down the ladder. When my foot hit the second step, light illuminated the area around me. The sudden change startled me and caused me to release my hold on the ladder. The ground came fast and hard.

The fall knocked the wind out of me. I scurried to my feet and waited for someone to appear. After a minute, I realized the lights were motion activated and relaxed a little. The room I had fallen into was cool and damp. The cool air felt good compared to Florida heat that waited for me up the ladder.

The round entryway of the bunker was six feet in diameter with nothing in it, and only one hallway leading deeper into the structure. I worked my way down the hall into the next room, which was huge. It had to be the size of a basketball court. Fluorescent lights lined the ceiling and let off a slight buzzing sound. The right side of the room was filled with shelves and weapon cases.

I reached down to open one four-foot-long green

container, and when the lid slid open, I saw the weapon it should contain was no longer present. The container only held black foam with the outline of a grenade launcher. The second case I opened had "AK-47" on the side. Like the first, it was empty. I opened the other ten cases along the wall of the bunker. Each was empty. All the guns had been cleared out.

My heart rate increased as I calculated the price of the weapons on the dark web. An AK-47 on the dark web went for around three thousand dollars. The military containers held around a hundred guns. Whoever had them—likely Juan—could clear three hundred thousand dollars off one container. With this much money, it might take years to stop him.

Maps were plastered across the wall above where the cases of guns lay. These maps were the only confirmation I needed that Juan had used Nebula to come after my family and that when Nebula failed to kill Sophie, Juan eliminated him. Each map corresponded to a house owned by Antonio's family or Zane's family. Juan planned to come after not only Sophie and me but also the people closest to us. I took out my phone and captured photos of the maps on the wall.

The middle of the room was filled with racks of MREs, jugs of water, and other consumables and first aid kits. The supplies were intact.

The far end of the room had been set up as a

computer station at one time. The monitors attached to the wall had been shattered. The computer's case had been pried open. The hard drives were gone. Whoever destroyed the place left nothing functioning.

When I had listened to Antonio's conversation, he mentioned the DVR drive might be readable. If CJ could pull the data off the drive, it might give us a lead on who destroyed the room and took the military weapons.

I glanced at my watch to calculate how long I had been down here. I had searched the bunker for the last hour.

Not finding anything that could lead to Juan sent a wave of defeat through my system. I had hoped Antonio's team had missed a clue. My husband's team was staffed with the best mercenaries, so I knew it was a long shot. But I needed to see this for myself. I grabbed a jug of water off the rack and whipped it across the room in frustration. It hit the map that showed our house with a thud. The map tore open and revealed a hidden safe. How fucking lucky could I be? I had given up hope that I would find anything useful.

The safe was a Winchester. I had cracked many safes in my time with the CIA, and a Winchester was a common one. I took a couple deep breaths and placed my ear against the safe. I slowly worked the dial of the safe until I felt the tumbler click. The first number hit at thirty-five. I turned the dial twice in the opposite direction, and the tumbler hit at five. Two numbers down, two to go. The third number missed, and I tried a couple more times before I felt the click. The last number came quick.

I grabbed the handle of the safe and turned it until the door popped open. Inside the safe lay a leather-bound book, which I took to the chair next to the computer station and flipped open. The first column had a coded name followed by a number and a date. The first entry was dated 2005. The last entry was the prior week.

I flipped through the book to see if I could decrypt the code. But I didn't see a pattern or find a key, so I placed the book under my arm. I walked back to the safe, closed the door. I pulled out my camera and took a few more pictures of the bunker to study at a later time.

The journey up the ladder went much better than my way down. I placed my gun and the book next to the bunker entrance and managed to close the door with a lot of effort. I used the grass from earlier to recover the door as well. On the way back to the car, I worked to cover my footsteps from earlier.

When I reached the car, I placed the leather book below my seat. I heard the click of a gun a few seconds before I felt the barrel press against my back. Fuck. Antonio was going to be mad.

9

ANTONIO

I rolled my neck to relieve the tension of the last month. The longer this case dragged on, the more nervous I was becoming. With any other case, the tension would roll off my shoulders. But with Kat and Sophie still in danger, the tension increased. Since the incident with her car and the men who tried to attack her at our house, I made sure she was armed at all times. I couldn't lose Kat again.

Stacy buzzed my phone to let me know Detective Higgins had arrived, then she told him to head back.

"Higgins. Good to see you." I greeted the big detective, who strode across the floor of my office and sat in the leather chair.

Asher must have heard the big detective enter the building. He was in my office before Detective Higgins had sat down. Higgins had worked with us in the past, and he knew anything he had to say to me could be said in front of my brother. From the look on Higgins's face, I wouldn't like the conversation.

"I wish I felt the same. How come every time we cross paths, you make my job harder? I need to know more about your supposed wife."

I had called Higgins because he was the best detective Ft. Lauderdale had to offer. But if he said one thing wrong or had something against Kat, he wouldn't make it out of this building. I glanced over at Asher, and it looked like he was thinking the same thing.

I took a swig of the coffee on my desk before I responded. "Supposed wife? She is my wife and has been for the past five years. You better think very carefully before you speak your next words."

Higgins frowned. "I ran Katherine Ross through the system, and I couldn't find anything. I also looked for your marriage license to see if the marriage was real."

Motherfucker. I planned to kill him slowly and feed this fucker to Kat's pet alligators. "For your information, the agency is working on fixing Kat's identity. If you spent this much time looking for who vandalized her car, we would know who did it by now."

"I pulled the CCTV videos from the street. The legal way. We were able to bring the man who vandalized Kat's car into custody. During the investigation,

Greg gave us some interesting information about your wife, which is why I'm here today."

Here was the reason Kat shouldn't go around killing people. If Greg had told the police that Kat killed his friend, we might be screwed. But Higgins hadn't brought police blazing in, so we might be okay. "What kind of information?"

"Your wife killed his friend with a garden gnome," Higgins said. I could see he was trying to hold back a laugh.

Fuck. That bastard ratted out my wife, but the story sounded so farfetched that Higgins didn't believe him.

"You saw my wife. She's tiny. Do you think she could take on Greg and his friend? With a garden gnome?" I asked, crossing my arms over my chest.

"I didn't believe the man's story. You know how things work. I needed to check out the story. But why is he after your wife?" Higgins asked.

"She is helping his wife, Lily, through the Ross Women's Outreach Center. He's an abusive asshole."

Greg needed to be taken out. *Fuck.* I sounded like my wife.

I needed to get in touch with Alex today and find out if his friend in Dallas had a job opening for Lily. Greg was going to be even more pissed since he was arrested for vandalizing Kat's car. If we got Lily out of state, it would make it harder for Greg to cause any problems.

"You need to let us know if he gets out," Asher said.

"He will more than likely make bail today," Higgins ground out, his square jaw tightening. "Men like him should have a special place in hell."

I would do anything to protect my wife, and that included taking this fucker out because he turned my wife in to the police. For the past week, I'd preached about going to the cops and doing everything above board in the case with Greg. But if Kat was in danger, I would do anything to protect her. Higgins and his men could show up to our house and look for evidence. They wouldn't find anything. Yesterday, the alligators that were in the backyard were moved to South Miami, miles from our house.

"What's wrong with him?" Higgins asked Asher, nodding his head toward Antonio.

"He's thinking," Asher said, "and he's about to come up with a plan. He's worried about Greg getting out on bail and coming after Kat."

Asher was close. I was worried we couldn't stop Kat from putting herself in danger. I reached for the cup of coffee on my desk and took a nice, long swig, enjoying the bittersweet liquid gold running down my throat.

"Do you need help to look for his friend?"

Higgins seemed like he would accept our help but then declined. "No, I can't imagine your wife killing anyone."

I shrugged. "She's a delicate flower."

I heard a snort from Asher's direction. He had used his hand to cover his mouth. The fucker was going to blow our cover.

Higgins narrowed his eyes. "I highly doubt you married a delicate flower. You and all your brothers are assholes and need strong women. But Kat doesn't seem like a woman who would kill someone."

That was one of the things that made her a great assassin for the CIA. Nobody expected a five-foot-three pixie to take down a three-hundred-pound man with her bare hands or, like the other night, with a garden gnome.

"You're right. My wife is strong and puts me in my place. I'm going to make sure she has a detail on her at all times. We are also going to put another bodyguard on Lily until everything dies down. I assume Greg is going to be upset that he was caught for vandalizing Kat's car. If we see anything on our end, we'll make sure to contact you right away."

Higgins cursed under his breath. "From the glint in your eye, I can tell you're bullshitting me. Try not to kill him if he comes after Kat or Lily."

"All I can promise is that I will do everything I can to protect my wife."

Higgins let out a sigh and headed for the door. "I'll let the brass know your wife didn't kill Greg's friend." Higgins put his hand on the doorknob. "I still might need to talk to her."

"Why?" *Dammit.* I didn't need Higgins digging into Kat's past. One glance at her folder, and he would be back to arrest her for Greg's missing friend.

"She is going to DC next week with her sister, Sophie. When she gets back, we can set up a meeting," I informed Higgins. We needed to solve the Juan case before we dealt with the other mess Kat had gotten herself into. Life with Kat was never fucking dull.

"Sophie is Zane Tucker's fiancé." It was smart of Asher to drop the Tucker name. No way could Higgins argue about Kat leaving town.

Higgins nodded that he understood. "I'll look forward to talking with your wife in two weeks. It would be nice to talk to the woman who thawed your heart made of ice."

Higgins strode out the door, and I turned on my twin the minute it slammed shut. "Fuck, that was close."

Asher rubbed the bridge of his nose. "I can't believe that fucker said Kat killed his friend. He admitted he came after her."

"We need to do more digging on this guy before he gets out on bail. Once he is out, let's track him down and get this taken care of."

"I thought you told your wife we were going to let the authorities handle the issue with Greg."

"Clearly, I was wrong. We don't want him telling anyone else what Kat did. Let's have CJ look into this friend to see if any family is going to start asking questions." I didn't need this shit on top of being worried about Juan coming after Kat. She was supposed to help the women at the shelter with self-defense, not take out their lowlife spouses.

Asher pulled out his phone and sent a text message. "CJ's pulling up everything we need. He should have a complete report for us by tomorrow. You understand taking time to pull this data will interfere with CJ looking for Juan?"

We needed another tech person to help sift through the information we had. I started to regret the decision to keep Sophie and Kat out of the op. Maybe it was time we brought them in and they helped us find Juan. That way, we would also have them at AA Security so we could keep an eye on them.

I let out a tired sigh. "I think we should have Sophie and Kat come in and help."

Asher tapped his shoe on the carpet. "The extra

eyes would be good, and we wouldn't have to put bodyguards on them during the day."

Kat would be excited tonight when I told her we needed her help on the case. I hope she didn't fight me about not being able to go to the shelter for a few weeks.

"How do you think Zane will feel about us using Sophie to help on the case?"

"I know he worries all day about her being at White Hat after what happened last week."

Juan had been quiet for too long. I knew he hadn't gone away. We needed to figure out what his plan was and get ahead of it.

When we had Juan and Greg behind us, I planned to surprise Kat with the wedding she deserved and to give Ant a brother or sister.

I walked to the window. The view of the city was spectacular from my office. Asher had the same view since his office was next to mine. I wondered if Kat would be happy staying in one location when we had Juan and Greg behind us. The thought of Kat at home and pregnant had my dick hard.

"Hey, we'll find him before anything happens to Kat or Sophie." Asher stepped up next to me. "You know I would do anything for my sister-in-law. Hell, Alex might be a dick and spend his time behind a computer, but I know he would help you if you needed it. We are family, and we stand by each other. No way are either of these fuckheads going to get their hands on Kat. Hell, she's too entertaining to not have around. CJ and I really don't want to go back to working with your grumpy ass. I've noticed a change in you since she's been around, and I like it, man."

I understood what Asher was saying. And I would do the same if CJ were in trouble.

Leaving the military to open my own security firm had been the best decision I had made. I got to work with my brother, and it made our relationship ten times stronger. The men that worked for me were like family. When I was in the Navy, I had my brothers in arms, and we would die for each other. But the family I created at AA Security was a bond we would hold for life.

The phone on my desk vibrated and brought me out of my thoughts. FBI Director Charles Westblack's name flashed across the screen.

Westblack and I had served on the same SEAL team for a couple years. He left the navy and joined the FBI, and worked his way up the ranks. Over the years, we had worked cases together and tried to catch up as much as we could. He called when he was in town so we could get a drink.

I swiped my finger across the phone to answer in speaker mode. "Director."

Westblack's deep voice boomed through the phone. "Antonio, I have a situation. We arrested a woman during an op this morning."

"I don't understand what that has to do with me."

But in the back of my head, I guessed who he meant. I didn't want to admit it out loud because I hoped I was wrong. Asher pulled out his phone and sent CJ a message. He must have come to the same conclusion.

"The lady in custody states she's your wife. Do you know a Katherine Ross? Because our database can't find this woman. She's a ghost."

"Yes, I have a wife by the name of Katherine Ross. I'm on my way down." I clicked off the phone. I didn't have time to answer the questions I knew Westblack would ask.

Asher's fingers flew across his phone. He didn't look up when he said, "Mom's picking Ant up from school. I have the family lawyer meeting us at FBI headquarters, and CJ is going to run AA Security while we are gone."

I loved my brother. "Let's go break my wife out of jail."

10

KAT

Two hours. That was how long they kept me in that room since we arrived at the FBI. I was taken from Nebula Brack's bunker and escorted straight to FBI headquarters. Nobody said a word to me, and I didn't offer any once the cuffs were slapped on my wrist.

The cold temperature of the room annoyed me. This tactic might work for someone who hadn't been tortured before. Six years earlier, before I met Antonio, I was captured by Yar-Mebrab, the head of a terrorist group called Jawid Shapoor. They spent hours using a whip on my body until I lost consciousness. When that didn't work, they tried to waterboard me. Last, they tried electrical shock. I was tortured for six days before I was able to get the drop on one of the guards when he thought I was weak.

I looked around the interrogation room. There was

a one-way mirror that blocked my view of the other side. I was sure the agents on the other side of the window were watching for a sign that I was close to my breaking point.

For the fifteenth time, I glanced at the clock on the wall. Ant needed to be picked up from school. Antonio would be called when I didn't answer or show up. *Fuck.* Antonio would be pissed when he found out I had been detained by the FBI. They would tell him I was at the bunker. He would want to know how I found out about it.

The metal door to the interrogation room swung open and banged against the wall. The agent was trying to get a rise out of me.

He looked familiar, but I couldn't quite place where I had seen him before. He was old for an agent. His hair was salt and peppered, and he had stress lines under his eyes. For his age, he was in shape and would intimidate a normal person. It had been a while since I had been interrogated. I thought I might have some fun until Antonio showed up.

"Katherine?" The agent's voice was deep and had a hint of a Southern drawl. "Do you know why you are here?" He folded himself into the metal chair across the table.

Did this guy really think I would just turn over my

information? This would be more fun than I originally planned.

"Nope. The agents didn't tell me why I was handcuffed and brought in."

"Are you really going to play it that way?" Agent No-Name laid the folder he held on the table and gave me his full attention.

The need to get out and back to my family was stronger than the fun of playing with Agent No-Name. "You want info, but I don't even know your name. From the TV shows I've watched, I know you're supposed to give me something for the information I have."

He nodded and tapped the folder on the table. "I'm Director Westblack. Now, tell me why you were in that bunker." He stared me down.

I shook my head. "Why is the Director of the FBI in Florida interrogating me? You ran my name and prints. What came up?"

Director Westblack was a friend of Antonio's. If my prints or information were in any system, he wouldn't be in the room with me. I knew my information wouldn't show up anywhere. The CIA didn't let their operatives' information appear in any database.

He leveled a glare at me. "Why do I have the feeling that you're more dangerous than you're letting on?" He pointed at the folder. "And you already know nothing came back on your prints or name. So I ask you again—why were you at Nebula Brack's bunker? Did you help with the arms sale?"

My eyebrows shot up in surprise, and the director cussed under his breath. I didn't know anything about an arms sale. They weren't after Nebula for the same reason we were after him.

"I don't know anything about a sale."

My hands were still cuffed to the table, and I indicated them with a nod. "Are these really necessary? I highly doubt I could take you down."

It would be hard, but I had faith that I could take him if necessary. But I wasn't going to cause issues with the FBI. I wanted to see if I could get more information out of him before I told him to call Antonio.

"I'm not sure that's safe." Westblack frowned. "You might be small, but you radiate a vibe that is dangerous." But he unlocked the cuffs, contradicting his own words with his actions.

Westblack cocked his head. "Time to start talking, Ms. Stewart. You also disrupted a planned raid. It looks like the bunker had been cleared out. I'll ask again, did you move the weapons."

Over the years, I had meant to go to the DMV and change my last name. The first time I'd gone, the line was wrapped around the building, so I kept driving. I hadn't made it back. Maybe it was time to get that done. It would make it easier when I got arrested.

Westblack was right. I needed to stop the game and get Antonio down here to get me out of this place.

"Ross."

"I don't understand. What does Ross mean?"

The director looked over his shoulder at the one-way mirror. He thought it meant something for his case.

"My last name is Ross, not Stewart." When he looked like he was going to say something, I continued. "My husband is Antonio Ross."

The director sprang from his chair and headed toward the door, pulling a cell phone out of his pocket on the way. Antonio would be with me soon.

ANTONIO

I gripped the wheel of the Range Rover while I swerved through traffic. My eyes never left the road, but I wasn't really paying attention to it. I had a mental picture of my wife in an interrogation room. What the hell did she do to get arrested by the FBI? It had to be something big if the director was involved. Kat was strong. She wouldn't take crap from him.

Ten minutes later, we pulled into the Miami FBI

building. "I can't believe my wife is being detained."

Asher raised his eyebrow. "You found your wife dragging a dead body across the lawn the other night. And you can't believe she's being detained by the FBI?"

I didn't respond to Asher right away. I headed toward the glass doors. "Let's find the director and break Kat out of here."

"Hopefully, we can break her out. We still don't know why she's here."

A million different scenarios ran through my head. In one, she had killed someone and gotten caught in the act. I swung the heavy bulletproof glass doors open and was hit with a cold blast of air. With a quick glance around the lobby, I spotted the receptionist desk. "I'm here to see Director Westblack."

"I'm sorry, sir. The director is not here. He works out of the DC office."

I grabbed my cell phone out of my pocket and redialed Westblack's number. He answered on the second ring. "I'm down in reception. According to them, you don't work here. If you don't work here, why do you have my wife?"

The phone clicked off on the other end. The director didn't respond to my question. The receptionist's phone rang immediately. Her face paled when she answered it, and her only words were "Yes, sir."

"He's on his way down," the receptionist whispered. I didn't care if he yelled at her. They had my wife.

Five minutes later, I saw Westblack exiting the elevator. "Where is she?"

Asher rested his hand on my shoulder. "You need to cool it, man."

I took a deep breath.

Westblack motioned for us to enter the elevator. He didn't say anything until the door closed. "Let's head to my office and talk, and then you can see your wife. I want to know why she was at my op location today."

There was no way I was going to be kept away from my wife any longer. "Not going to happen. I want to see Kat now."

"You are a pain in my ass. We'll grab her on the way to my office."

The second Westblack unlocked the interrogation door with his code, I swung the door open. Kat's eyes landed on me, and she bolted from the chair. Our arms wrapped around each other. It felt good to have her in my arms. I grabbed her and led her out of the room.

The director didn't look amused. "If you two are done, I want answers."

A couple minutes later, Asher, Kat, and I were seated at the conference table in the director's office.

He got straight to the point. "Now, tell me what you were doing in Nebula's bunker."

Fuck. Kat had gone to a radical's bunker without backup. I was going to tan her hide when we got home. We still didn't know if Nebula's other men came back to that area even though we had kept up satellite surveillance of the area around the bunker. But it seemed that since we'd left Kat out of the investigation, she just put herself in more danger.

Kat looked at the glass of water that sat in front of her. Then she looked at the one-way mirror. Then she looked back at the table. She looked everywhere but at me. No, she wasn't going to get away without explaining herself, and at the moment, I didn't care what the director heard. She had better have a good reason for why she went to that bunker.

"Kat, how did you know about that bunker?" I asked, trying to keep my voice level.

Kat held up her hands in defense. "You were keeping me out of the investigation. I want him dead, and I'm sick of waiting. The other day, I bugged your jacket and listened to your conversations."

I wished she hadn't admitted to wanting to kill someone in front of the director of the FBI.

"What investigation?" Westblack asked.

Asher shrugged. "It's classified."

"Do any of you know where Nebula is?"

"Dead," Kat blurted out before Asher and I could come up with a story. We didn't want to have to drag the director into the op.

Westblack raised his dark brow, waiting for more. "That's all I get? Dead."

Fuck. "We're working on a case for the president. Can we leave it at that?"

"I don't care whose operation you are running. We are missing a truck full of military weapons. My main concern is protecting the people in this country. Now, someone tell me who might have the weapons if Nebula is dead."

"Juan Sanchez." Bitterness flooded my mouth every time I said his name.

"You're telling me the ex-director of the CIA stole the weapons and killed Nebula."

That summed up as much as I wanted him to know. "Yes. If we find any leads on the weapons, we will send them your way. We are after Juan."

Director Westblack let out a sigh. "Fine, but why do I have the feeling that you're not going to send me what I need until your operation is over?"

The director was spot on. I wouldn't send him anything until we had Juan. That didn't mean I wouldn't send him all the information he needed after we had him.

I grabbed Kat's hand and led her from the FBI

building. I heard Asher's steps behind us. So much was rushing through my mind. Kat had been detained by the FBI, and Juan had an enormous pile of military weapons.

ASHER TOOK a taxi out to Nebula's bunker to retrieve Kat's rented SUV. As I drove home with Kat, I was fuming over how she had put herself in danger. What would have happened if one of Nebula's men had been down in the bunker? They would have killed her before I noticed she was gone.

I glanced at the time. It was past five. In the passenger seat, Kat sat looking out the window. Most of the time, I could read her thoughts. But not this time. Her shoulders were hunched over, and I heard a slight sniffle come from her direction.

"What's wrong, Kat?"

She whipped her hand across her face to remove the tears. "I'm sorry. I didn't plan to go alone."

She shouldn't have gone at all. "Kat." I collected my thoughts for a second. "Why didn't you come to me? If you wanted to go, I would've gone with you. Instead, you went to the hideout of a possible terrorist organization by yourself. Did you ever stop to think that he might have men that work for him?" I pounded my fists on the steering wheel. "Hell, Kat, even Asher didn't go there alone. He took Zane."

"I know. I fucked up."

The final few minutes of the car ride were filled with silence. When the wheels stopped in the driveway, Kat didn't wait for me to turn off the car. She was halfway to the door by the time I stepped out.

"Kat, stop," I demanded.

She stopped at the door and turned at my words. "Fuck you, Antonio." She proceeded to enter the house and slam the door.

Jesus, this woman was going to drive me crazy. I opened the front door and glanced through the rooms until I found Kat curled up on our bed in tears. I climbed onto the other side and pulled her into my arms. I rubbed circles on her back while she cried. "Kitty Kat, I'm not mad at you. Disappointed, yes. Scared, hell yes. Mad, no. I lost you once, and I don't want that to happen again."

"I hate... the look... in your eye... when you're disappointed... in me." She hiccupped.

I pulled Kat close to my body. "There are going to be times when we're mad or disappointed in each other, but we have to talk and work through our problems. Keeping our feelings bottled up and not talking about them will destroy our relationship."

She didn't respond for a couple of heartbeats. "I

was on my own for so long. I knew the second I stepped out of the car it was a mistake, but I couldn't stop myself."

"Next time, call me. I will stop whatever I'm doing, and we can go dig through a bunker or jump out of a plane. Hell, if you have a good reason, I'll help you rob a bank, but I want to do it together."

"Okay. Antonio?" Her voice was hopeful.

"Yes, Kitty Kat?"

"I want to be more involved in the case."

"Asher and I were talking about getting your help and Sophie's on the case before I received the call from Director Westblack." I felt her body tense under my hands. "We had decided we needed both of you."

Kat jumped onto my lap and straddled me. Her hands wrapped around the back of my head, and she pulled me up for a kiss. Before she had time to end it, I weaved my hand through her red locks and held her in place. Her hips started to grind against me. When we finally pulled back, we both were panting.

I worked her T-shirt over her head. A white lace bra was wrapped around her chest. I pulled her back in for a kiss while I worked the strap free. I cupped both of her breasts with my hands. When I pinched her nipples, she let out a groan.

Kat rolled over onto her back. In no time, I worked her jeans down her legs, and she spread herself for me.

I slid my shoulders under her legs and licked. She was already wet and needy. The more I sucked on her clit, the wetter she became.

"More, Antonio. Please."

I flattened my tongue and ran it over her clit. Kat jumped at the rough sensation. "Kat, you respond to my touch so eagerly." I continued to lick her nub. With each lick, she arched her body off the bed, and she tried to get me to move faster.

"Ant—" Her words were cut off as I pressed two fingers into her folds. A loud moan escaped her mouth instead of the end of my name.

She was near the edge. I worked my fingers faster and took her bundle of nerves into my mouth. As I sucked, I was rewarded with the sound of my name screamed from her lips. I loved nothing more than to hear Kat scream my name when she went over the edge.

I slowly licked her juices as she came out of her orgasm-induced coma. When her eyes landed on me, the love in them amazed me.

"Turn over, Kitty Kat."

Kat flipped at my command. She placed a pillow under her head and shifted her legs, so her ass was in the air. I grazed my hand over her plump ass. "Your ass is perfect, Kitty Kat."

The view of Kat with her ass in the air had me so

hard that it was almost painful. I leaned down and took another lick of Kat's plump folds. Her knees trembled with each additional lick. She was ready for me. I lined myself up and slowly worked my member in.

In that position, I could go so much deeper. I ran my hands over her back as I worked in each inch. I had to pause to collect myself, but Kat didn't want to wait. She pushed herself back and took my full girth. We both moaned in pleasure. I clenched my teeth and pulled back. God, my wife was perfect.

Kat tried to quicken the pace, but I wanted it to last. I grabbed hold of her hips to slow her down. She started to rub her clit. The view of my wife losing control was breathtaking.

"You feel so fucking good." I licked my finger and ran it over Kat's anal star. The single touch sent Kat over the edge. I could feel her channel suck me in farther. I couldn't hold back. I thrust in and out of her at the pace of man going over the edge. When I felt my balls tighten, I pushed in deep. Neither of us moved from our position.

Kat's breathing leveled out, so I rolled to the side and pulled her into my arms. When she snored softly, I slid out of bed to go work. For now, my wife is safe, but for how long?

11
KAT

"Who are all these people?" I hated large social gatherings. Too many people made me itch. For so many years, it was just me and Ant. Antonio's family was so large that it felt overwhelming at times.

"It took me a long time to get used to the size of this family." Bridget waved her hand at the crowd of people in Mr. and Mrs. Ross's backyard. Family and friends were gathered to welcome Antonio's little sister, Alison, back from her last assignment with Doctors Without Borders. She had been placed in Kabul, Afghanistan.

Antonio said he didn't think she would be back longer than a month. She had been gone for the past two years, jumping from one location to another. But Alison had wanted to come back and meet her nephews.

Aaron, the youngest of the four Ross brothers, had also shown up to the gathering. He had just finished filming another blockbuster movie. The four brothers stood in the corner, joking with each other. Bridget and CJ had joined me on the patio. Sophie and Zane were supposed to be here any minute. Ant ran around in the grass with his cousins.

"I don't know if I will ever get used to this," CJ added. He reached for his IPA and took a long swig.

The party was a nice distraction from what was happening in our lives. It was filled with joy and happiness.

"Hey, there's Neal and Daisy." Bridget pointed to the couple crossing the lawn toward the Ross brothers. "Let's go grab Daisy before she's stuck listening to the guys for the next hour."

I stared at the couple and contemplated if walking through the crowd was worth talking to Daisy. It was. Daisy was the sunshine to anyone's dark days. She had been captured and forced to live as a sex slave for years. Before she was captured, she did makeup for the stars out in Hollywood. She left that life and friends behind and hadn't seen any of them since.

Bridget, CJ, and I made it to the group the same time Neal and Daisy did.

"Daisy, I would like you t—" Neal's words were cut off.

"Lucy Ivy, is that you? Why did you disappear?" Aaron ripped Daisy out of Neal's arms and had her in a hug before Neal had time to react.

It didn't take long. Neal yanked Daisy out of Aaron's arms, and she fell back into Neal's chest. Neal's jaw was clenched. "I think you are mistaken, Aaron. Next time you want to give Daisy a hug, you ask first."

Daisy twisted and placed her hand on Neal's chest. "Master, it's okay. Daisy does know Aaron. Daisy used to do his makeup for the movies, when I went by the name Lucy." Daisy turned back to Aaron while keeping her hand on Neal. "It's nice to see you, Aaron. I no longer go by Ivy. Daisy is my name, and Neal is my master. He's a good master, not like the one that tortured me in Hollywood."

I heard Neal groan. Daisy's filter was lacking in social settings.

Aaron stepped toward Daisy but stopped short when Neal pulled her closer into him. Daisy let out a laugh that made everyone smile. "Master, can we talk with Aaron in private? He is an old friend."

Neal nodded, and the three left the circle of friends to talk.

"Damn. The conversation was just getting interesting," CJ quipped.

Antonio cleared a path for me back to the outdoor

patio. The evil Florida sun started to set, which caused the temp to drop two whopping degrees. I sat down on the outdoor couch.

"Stay with me."

Antonio joined me on the sofa, but his eyes never left the crowd.

"What are you looking for?"

He pulled me onto his lap and wrapped his arms around me. "Something doesn't feel right. It's probably nothing, but I feel eyes on us."

At Antonio's words, I saw Asher search the crowd of people, and I looked for something out of the ordinary myself.

Juan hadn't done anything for over a month. I had started to think he was gone. "I think we keep waiting for something to happen, and the longer it takes, the tenser we all become. Maybe Juan decided to take the money he had left and go into hiding."

Antonio went still. "That's what he wants us to think. He's going to wait until we drop our guard."

"I wish he were dead," CJ said, his tone exasperated. "It's getting to be a lot of work to run our main ops plus scan for Juan."

"It won't be much longer," Asher said. He was an optimist, but his eyes studied the backyard intently.

Movement at the back of the lawn caught my attention. I strained to see what it was. Then a group of kids ran through the bushes. I breathed heavily. Antonio's suspicion had my nerves on high alert.

"We need to stop talking about Juan and enjoy the party. Looks like Neal no longer wants to kill your brother."

The corners of Antonio's lips twitched. "Neal needed a kick in the ass to move things along with Daisy. Maybe he'll feel threatened by Aaron and get a move on."

The three were sitting in a set of chairs on the side porch with Daisy in the middle. Daisy's smile was spread across her face.

Asher tipped his beer bottle in the trio's direction. "They all seem to be getting along."

Daisy deserved someone who would worship her. From the look of the three talking, she might end up with two men.

Antonio's phone rang. His dark brow rose when he looked at the screen. He leaned over and kissed me on the forehead before he answered the call. He went to the other side of the patio, so I couldn't hear what he said into the phone. But I could see the tension in his shoulders. It didn't look good for whoever was on the other side of the call.

I glanced at Asher but watched every move Antonio made. He seemed to be bothered by the phone call.

The call could be about any case. AA Security had hired two more employees in the past month. The security company was up to ten mercenaries, and they were all deployed on assignments at the moment. But my Spidey sense told me it had to do with Juan.

I picked at the label on the beer bottle. Antonio's movement became animated. "Asher, any idea what that call's about?"

"No, but it doesn't look good."

"Maybe one of the new guys messed up a case?"

Asher looked away from Antonio. "If there was an issue at work, they would've called me, because everyone is too scared to mess up and tell Antonio. They think I'm a buffer."

I had never understood why people feared Antonio. He was like a giant, sexy teddy bear I enjoyed stripping naked. I wanted to know who he was talking to.

"Can either of you read lips?" I waved my hand in Asher and CJ's direction. They both shook their heads. "Have I ever mentioned that I don't like being kept out of the loop?"

Antonio hung up the phone after ten minutes. By the time he returned, my mind had run a million scenarios. One scenario that scared me a lot was that something had happened to Sophie.

Antonio reached up to wipe his eye, then sat down

and pulled me into his arms. "What was that call about?" I asked, my voice shaking.

Something had happened. Something spectacularly bad. He didn't reply, just pulled me in tighter to his chest.

Neal chose this moment to come up to the patio with Daisy following behind. He stopped and surveyed our faces before he dropped down into the last seat. Daisy took her place on his lap.

"What's going on?"

"There's been an accident," Antonio gritted out.

The only way Antonio would be this upset about an accident was if it involved someone close to him. Otherwise, he would have told everyone what happened the second he got off the phone. Instead, he pulled me into his arms and kissed the back of my neck.

"Was it Sophie?" I choked out.

Antonio gripped my waist tighter.

"Was it Sophie?" I yelled.

Guests turned our direction to see what was happening.

Antonio moved me off his lap. He stood up, looked at Asher, and nodded. When he looked toward the back patio doors, there was a mixture of weariness and remorse in his eyes, and I hated it. I needed him to say the words. His shoulders slumped, and he ran a hand across his brow.

Asher and CJ were on their feet. Everyone seemed to be on high alert, and Antonio still hadn't told me what had happened to my sister.

"What happened?" I demanded again.

His eyes shifted to the side of the crowd. Asher must've picked up on the cue, because he took off in the direction Antonio indicated. I didn't pay much attention to where Asher was going. I just wanted to know what happened to Sophie.

Antonio's eyes pinned me, making dread come to the forefront.

"There was an accident."

It was bad. Whatever had happened was really bad, and it was about me or Sophie, or he would've told me the second the phone call ended.

"Please tell me," I begged.

"You're going to be mad at me for what I'm about to tell you," he whispered.

"Fucking tell me!" I needed the words to be said out loud. I needed Antonio to tell me what had happened. If the accident was bad, he would have led with that.

"Sophie was killed in a car accident." Antonio spoke each word slowly so I could process it.

From the look on his face during the call and afterward, I had been prepared for him to tell me something had happened to Sophie. But when the words hit me, the hot, humid Florida air left my lungs. Sophie had become my best friend again. Who was going to be Ant's aunt? Zane would be devastated. I needed more details. "How?"

"She and Zane were driven off the road. She died on impact, and the paramedics pronounced her dead moments ago."

My knees went weak. It took everything in me to stay standing. Nausea rolled around in my stomach.

"Antonio, what are you doing?" CJ asked. "This isn't the place to tell her something like that."

Antonio said something, but my mind couldn't comprehend the words. The only thing my mind could do was recall pictures of my perfect sister. She hadn't deserved to be killed.

Juan needed to be destroyed. I would draw his death out for days and make it painful and cruel.

The one man I counted on as I grew up was coming after me and everyone that meant something to me. He'd never given me a chance to live a happy life. The instant I started to see what happiness was, Juan ripped it from my grasp.

Who would he go after next? Antonio or Ant? Nausea rolled through me again at the thought of someone hurting my baby. A sob caught in my throat.

What if Juan went after more than my close friends and family? Daisy and Neal could be in danger just for being near me. The women at the shelter might be on his radar. Was anyone near me safe? Sophie was already gone. I couldn't lose anyone else.

The only way to stop Juan was to turn myself over to him. I couldn't stand for anyone else to be hurt because of me. I was never meant to have the "happily ever after" I've seen on TV or read about in books.

At least Ant would be happy with Antonio. They would miss me for a while before they both moved on.

With the decision made, a calm settled over me. I had already lost my sister. I couldn't lose anyone else. Hopefully, Juan would be happy with me and leave my remaining family alone. I turned toward the exit. It was time to confront my uncle.

"Kat?" Antonio's voice rang out. But I didn't stop. He wouldn't have understood what I needed to do.

A shiver went down my spine as I thought about what Juan might do to me. I planned to contact all his known associates, letting him know I was ready to come in. Would he take me out with one bullet, or would he make me go back to work for him? If it kept Antonio and Ant safe, I would do anything. I had experienced true happiness for the past two months with Antonio. Maybe that was all I could have.

"Katherine!"

I turned and headed for the car. The mass of bodies caused my anxiety to spike. I took a deep breath to stay calm. I needed to stay calm. The parking lot was in sight. Antonio kept speaking to me from behind. When I made it to the car, I would head north and talk with anyone I could find in New York. Someone had to know where Juan was.

"Kat, you need to stop." Antonio wrapped his muscular arms around my waist, stopping my progress to the car.

"Let me go!" I screamed and kicked back.

The only thing I cared about was keeping Antonio and Ant safe. I needed to stop Juan, and I was the only one that could do it. He wanted me.

"I can't." Antonio swung me over his shoulder. "You're my everything, and I won't let you sacrifice yourself."

I couldn't hold back the sob. "He wants me. Let me save everyone else from getting hurt. You have to let me go."

"You are not going to sacrifice yourself, damn it." Antonio ignored my protest. He walked toward the door and looked back at Neal. "Find Asher and CJ and have them meet me in my father's study. I want you and Daisy in there too."

No matter how much I wiggled and moved, I couldn't break free from Antonio's hold. "You have to let me go, Antonio. I can't stand the thought of something happening to you or Ant. What happens if he goes after our friends or Asher? Do you want to lose your brother?"

"Nobody's going to take Asher or me out. You need to trust me." Antonio continued in the direction of the office in the Ross mansion.

"It's too late. He already got my sister. How can you just stand here and do nothing? He killed my sister, my last living family member. Don't you understand why I need to do this?"

Antonio walked into his father's office and set me down on the brown leather sofa. When I went to say something, he put a finger over his mouth, motioning for me to stop talking. "Stay put." He leaned in and whispered in my ear. "I will explain everything soon."

He pulled a device out of his father's desk that looked like a walkie-talkie and switched the device on. He didn't look my way. Instead, he walked around the office, waving the device over every square inch.

When he waved it over his father's desk, it made a loud beep noise. Antonio flipped the laptop over and unscrewed the bottom panel. From underneath the panel, he pulled out a device the size of a dime and stomped on it.

His father's office was bugged. Juan had been in here.

Antonio made a couple more passes through the office. He looked like he was ready to tear someone apart.

Antonio joined me on the couch and pulled me into his arms. "I'm sorry. I need you to forgive me."

"You couldn't stop Juan. Why are you sorry?" Tears started to run down my face. The shock from earlier was dying down, and my emotions were going all over the place.

"You need to forgive me, Kitty Kat. He was watching. Zane and I needed your emotions to be believable. I didn't want to do it this way, But Zane and I needed to make a quick decision."

Why did he say "believable"? Did that mean Sophie was okay?

"I need you to spell this out for me, Antonio."

"I had to lie to you. Juan was on the other side of the fence, watching. Asher and CJ went after him."

"Lie? Sophie didn't get into an accident?"

"Yes, Sophie and Zane got into an accident, but Sophie didn't die in the crash. When the paramedics came, Zane decided to fake Sophie's death and send her to a safe house. He couldn't handle her being in harm's way again. I'm sorry I lied to you, Kitty Kat. It ripped me apart to see you cry. But Juan was watching."

I didn't have time to ask more questions, and I

didn't know how I felt about Antonio lying to me. Asher, CJ, Neal, and Daisy came into the office. Asher's face was red with anger.

"That fucker had a helicopter!" Asher yelled. CJ had taken a seat at Mr. Ross's desk, and his fingers were flying across the keyboard of the laptop.

I felt as though it was all too much to take in, and I wanted to see Sophie. I needed to see her with my own eyes.

"I want to see Sophie now," I said to the room.

Antonio frowned. "Kat, she's at a safe house."

"I don't care if she's on the fucking moon. I want to see her now."

I wasn't sure I would ever be able to forgive Antonio for playing off my biggest fear.

12

KAT

I looked around Sophie's room in the safe house. Zane had whisked Sophie away to one of the numerous houses he owned under different shell companies. It wasn't the largest home he owned, but it wasn't your house next door.

The house had to be close to six thousand square feet and sat on ten acres. When I walked up the marble-tiled grand staircase to Sophie's room, I passed a surveillance room most techies would drool over. Every square inch of the property was under surveillance. Zane had lasers programmed to detect the slightest vibration in the ground.

Three men I had never seen before manned the computers in the surveillance room. Zane and Antonio sat at the conference room table in the room, going over Juan's last move.

Of course, even with all the technology in the world, no one could make the worry in my stomach go away. I thought I had lost my sister again. It had been three days since she and Zane had been run off the road and Antonio had told me she died. Deep down, I understood why Zane and Antonio decided to lie to me, but that didn't mean I agreed with them. Antonio hadn't needed to listen to Zane when he asked Antonio to fake Sophie's death. He could've told me something else that would've made me cry and put on a scene.

As I walked across the plush carpet, Sophie's head turned from the TV mounted on the wall in the bedroom. "When are you going to forgive him?" she asked. Wow. No "Hi" or "How are you doing?" Just straight to the point.

I reached the king-size bed and sat next to Sophie. "Sophie... I don't know. Those two made a choice that devastated me. They told me you died. Could you forgive Zane if he told you I died to put on a show?"

Her frown deepened, and she leaned over to grab a pint of ice cream she had been eating. "I was in on the decision. Are you angry with me?" Sophie had a cut under her eye from when the glass shattered in the accident. Her movements were stiff from the seatbelt bruise.

I took a second to think about it before answering. "I should be, but I was so happy you were alive that I didn't care. It hurts that the people I love most can wound me like that. He could've told me someone else had died to make me cry. Fuck, Sophie, I thought I had lost you and that Juan was coming for everyone I care about."

"I'm sorry." Sophie let out a sniffle. "We weren't thinking about what it would do to you. Zane and I looked at it as a way to get something over on Juan. Did you see Zane's black eye?"

It was the first thing I'd noticed when Zane answered the door. "Was that from the accident?"

Sophie flipped through a few more channels before landing on an old episode of *House Flippers*. "No. Antonio punched him when he showed up to work yesterday. He said that was for upsetting his wife. Have you looked at your husband? He looks like someone killed his puppy, ran it over, and set it on fire."

What she said was true. Antonio had tried everything to make me speak to him. Being angry with Antonio was hard, and I missed his touch. Without Antonio by my side, I tossed and turned all night, wishing Antonio had his arms wrapped around me, letting me know everything would work out. His touch helped soothe the anxiety that coursed through my body.

If anything, the incident with Zane and Sophie

should have made me want to be around Antonio more. I could lose him any day.

I had gone years with no close family around. My sixteenth birthday was the last time Juan and I had spent a holiday together. He took me to a nice restaurant and informed me that I would be moving to a new school. I was devastated to learn I was going to have to leave the life I was used to.

A limousine picked us up from the restaurant, and in the back sat two of my suitcases. I recognized them the second I got in the car. Juan directed the driver in the opposite direction of his mansion in Dulles, Virginia. The car took us to a remote airstrip. Juan didn't even exit the car. Two men in black suits opened the door and asked me to step out. That was the last time I saw my uncle for two years.

The men led me to a helicopter as tears streamed down my face. I didn't understand what was happening. Later, I learned "the Farm" at the CIA's Camp Peary was to be my new home. Camp Peary got the name "the Farm" during World War II when the War Department commandeered a few farms to make a facility to train officers.

It should've been called Camp Hell. The CIA used it to develop the next generation of agents. The first year, when I was sixteen, I learned to speak Madarin and Arabic. Instructors at the farm taught me how to pick locks and change my identity. That was the year I homed in on my sniper skills. Even though I was the youngest agent, I had the best shot.

In my second year, everything changed. I was taught how to withstand torture. One of the training exercises I would never forget was called "stress position." My instructor handcuffed my feet to an eye bolt in the floor and my hands above my head. They made me hold the position for over forty hours. When I was released, I collapsed to the ground from muscle failure. I went through things no sixteen-year-old should ever have to see or endure.

Sophie pushed me to get my attention. I had been so lost in remembering that dreadful time that I hadn't heard anything she was saying. "Sorry. I was lost in the past."

"You know, we've never really talked about what you had to go through. The stories about when you were an assassin are interesting, but what was it like when you were younger?"

"I missed my family. Juan hired people to take care of me." I took a deep breath. "When I turned sixteen, he turned me over to the CIA."

Sophie sat up and gave me her full attention. "How could someone do something so evil to family?"

"He knew his stepsister had two genius kids. Juan

played the long game and did pretty well for quite a few years, if you think about it."

Sophie frowned and handed me the tub of chocolate chip ice cream. "I can't wait until he's underground. Did you make any friends through the process, or were you alone for all those years?"

I had lived with Juan for ten years before being shipped to the CIA. He hadn't let me leave the house except for school. I had friends at school but none at home. The nannies he hired were evil bitches whom he paid to torment me. They would lock me in my room or go days without giving me food when I was younger.

The Farm didn't have anyone my age. Everyone was in their twenties. Nobody hung out with the sixteen-year-old, so I spent all my time alone. "I didn't leave any friends behind. Antonio was my first best friend when I became a field agent. But let's not talk about Juan for once. Are you working from here until everything blows over?"

Sophie pointed to the laptop on the bed. "I'm working on helping a company increase their cybersecurity."

Computers were never my thing. "Does Zane have people here during the day when he's gone?"

"Yes, and they watch me like a hawk. I know it's serious, and I don't plan on leaving. Bridget will let me work remotely as long as I need to."

"I'm happy she is letting you work from here. I'm heading back to the women's center next week."

I loved to help the women. Antonio promised I could go back next week as long as I took a bodyguard. We had compromised on a female bodyguard from Brock's security company. Mia wouldn't intimidate the women like Antonio's men might.

The bedroom door opened, and Antonio and Asher entered. Antonio looked hot in a tight black shirt that stretched around his biceps. But the wariness in his eyes made my heart break. He didn't know if he was welcome. When I patted the seat next to me on the bed, he practically ran to my side. Zane joined Sophie on the other side.

Antonio leaned over and kissed my forehead. "I missed you, Kitty Kat," he whispered so only I could hear.

"Any leads?" Sophie asked.

"The pilot of Juan's helicopter, a man named Weiss, was in the military at the same time as Nebula. When we dug further, they both deployed to Iraq together."

"They were in the same unit?" I asked. Antonio ran his hand down my side. His touch made me feel grounded for the first time in days.

"Yes. We're trying to get a list of the full unit. The

mission they were on was declared highly classified by Juan," Zane said with a sigh.

"Doesn't your clearance give you access?" Zane and Antonio had the highest clearance appointed by the president, so they shouldn't have had a problem getting the info.

Antonio frowned as he pulled me into his arms. "We have as-high-as-you-can-get security clearance and can look at anything on the government servers. The issue we are running into is that the data from that deployment is missing."

"Then how do you know they were in the same unit?" Sophie had asked the question that was on the tip of my tongue. If they were able to find the information linking Weiss the helicopter pilot and Nebula, why couldn't they pull the remaining unit information?

Zane flipped the channel from HGTV to the NBA finals game. "CJ tracked the helicopter and then pulled the flight plan. Asher broke into Weiss's house yesterday and found a photo of the unit. I recognized the place in Iraq where it was taken. We don't know anyone else in the photo. Neither name is in any military database."

Antonio's eyes tightened. "We think Juan used a unit to run missions for him off the books. Juan deleted the unit's information from the servers years ago. We need to figure out who all the men in the photo are.

Clearly, if they are working for him now, they knew he was corrupt when he worked for the CIA."

The more they dug into Juan, the more hurdles and missing pieces they found. "I know Neal was working on a new facial recognition software. He might be able to use the photo to find the man we're looking for." I motioned to Zane. "If your brother approves, he could run it against one of NSA's satellites, and we could locate them faster. Neal tried to run Juan, but I have a feeling Juan is wearing a disguise."

Antonio laced his fingers with mine and gave my hand a squeeze. "You are correct. He is wearing a disguise. I almost didn't recognize him at my parents' house. Zack gave us permission to do whatever it takes to get answers. We can send Neal the photo, and he can run all the men. If we find one, it might help us find Juan faster."

Zane pulled his phone out of his pocket. His fingers flew across the screen, and when he sent the text, his phone made a *whoosh* sound. "I asked Asher to send the picture to Neal."

It felt good to be in Antonio's arms again. When I lifted myself so I could sit on his lap, I was rewarded with the feeling of his hard member through his jeans. I squirmed in his lap and elicited a groan. His arms wrapped around my waist tighter to keep me still.

A smile split Zane's face. "Happy to see you're not mad at Antonio anymore."

Sophie got up from the bed and grabbed Zane's hand. "Let's go work on lunch."

Zane jumped up, grabbed Sophie around her waist, and threw her over his shoulder. A loud squeal erupted from her mouth. "But I want you for lunch." They exited the room in fits of laughter.

"Did you have fun talking to Sophie?" Antonio asked. He still ran his hand up and down my side.

"It was nice to catch up. I wish she didn't have to hide out until we find Juan. What if it takes months for us to find him?" I wanted Sophie to come to the women's center with me.

Patience. I needed patience to get through this. That was why I liked missions where the evidence clearly showed what the bad guy did. Then the CIA would tell me where my kill location was, and I could take my target out. I had never spent months looking for my targets. This cat-and-mouse game was getting old.

"We could skip lunch and head home," Antonio whispered. "The past few days of not holding you at night or getting a kiss in the morning has killed me. Let's go home, Kitty Kat, so I can make love to my wife for the rest of the day."

Antonio captured my lips. He ran his hand

through my hair, pulling me in tighter. I couldn't get enough of him. He seemed to need to show dominance and take over the kiss. His tongue swiped across my lips, requesting entrance. When he leaned back and broke the kiss, it was too soon. I wanted to stay locked to his lips.

13

KAT

It had been a full week since the attack on Sophie and Zane. Sophie was still at the safe house. Zane worked remotely, and so did Antonio. It had been nice to have him home with me the past few days.

Ant was on spring break and had been home from school. Antonio was worried about letting us out of the house. So we played games and binge-watched movies on Netflix. On one of the days, Lily came over and brought her son to play with Ant. They spent hours in Ant's room, where they played cops and robbers. Ant used to play assassin and bad guy, but Antonio thought we set a bad precedent with that game.

It was nice to see Ant make friends so easily. Once Lily's husband was behind bars and Juan was dead, Ant and Tommy could play together more often. Lily looked to be doing better. She wouldn't stop thanking us for having Jacob watch over her. Greg had tried to contact her numerous times, and Jacob stopped him each time. Alex Ross had talked with one of his friends and tried to help find Lily a job as a receptionist, but we hadn't heard back yet.

For the past few hours, I had worked on cleaning the house. Ant's grandparents had shown up and taken him to their house for the weekend. Antonio had been in his office for the last few hours, looking over the case files. Asher had recently gotten intel that led us to believe Juan had surfaced in Fort Lauderdale.

I was frustrated that we were always one step behind Juan. Neal had used his facial recognition software to identify three of the other men in Nebula's unit. The men had often met at a biker bar in South Miami. Antonio had sent Asher there to scope out the place and was able to get intel that there would be a meeting in two days.

Neal and Zane had been in constant contact and had come up with a game plan to take Juan and his men down. But I couldn't stop feeling it was going to be a diversion. Juan had been careful not to get caught for the last two months. I kept asking myself why he would make it so easy for us to discover when this meeting was going to take place.

CJ had retrieved partial video from the DVR player in the bunker. The video didn't add anything we didn't know. It was recorded video of inside the bunker. The video showed Juan meeting with the seven men of the military unit. We wondered if these men knew Juan had killed their friend.

I needed a distraction from my current thoughts. I grabbed a piece of paper and started to think about Ant's sixth birthday. It would be the first party Ant would celebrate with his dad and Antonio's family.

I glanced around the room, trying to figure out what I was going to do for a sixth birthday party. My eyes landed on Ant's cop action figure on the end of the table. Ant loved to play detective. We could set up a whole theme with his friends and have them figure out different cases.

I heard Antonio's feet pad across the living room carpet. Over the past couple of months, I'd gotten used to having Antonio in my life. I enjoyed my evenings cuddling up in his arms on the couch. The nights that we shared were the best memories. I would cherish them forever.

It was nice to have someone on my side who fought for me.

The more Antonio helped with parenting, the more I realized how much help I needed. And I wasn't the only one who needed help. Ant had blossomed so much since Antonio had been around. I didn't realize how much he'd needed a male figure in his life.

I didn't have to turn around to know that Antonio stood behind me. I could feel his presence.

"Are you and Zane done planning for the day?" I asked while I wrote my list of things we needed for Ant's birthday. Laser tag needed to go on the list.

Antonio took the chair next to me. "Is laser tag for the adults or the kids?"

I could only imagine the trouble Antonio and his brother's friends would get into if we had laser tag for the adults. But I had to admit that it would have been pretty fun to pit the guys against the girls.

"They were going to be for Ant's friends, but maybe we need to have a set for the adults as well."

He pulled the piece of paper from my hand. "I like your idea of a detective birthday party. I'm so proud of you Kitty Kat. I thought you wanted an assassin birthday party."

I winced at his declaration.

"You were originally going to have an assassin birthday party, right?"

"Maybe." I pointed to the piece of paper that he stole from my hands. "But as you can see, I'm going to be mother of the year. When 'assassin' came to mind, I looked around the room for an idea and landed on Ant's cop figurine."

His lips curved slightly, and in the dining room light, I could see the smile he tried to hide. "You're the best mom there is. Maybe we could have a detective looking for the assassin."

"I appreciate that, Antonio, but I think we're going to do a detective looking for a bank robber." I got up from the dining room table and headed to the fridge for a drink. Ant would be at his grandparents' house for the weekend. We would spend the following day finalizing the plan to go after Juan. The takedown was supposed to happen Sunday night.

"Wine or beer?" I asked from the fridge. I had planned to crack open a bottle of Moscato.

"Beer."

When I joined Antonio back at the table, he pulled me onto his lap. A wave of need hit my body when I felt Antonio's hard member press against my back. Antonio wrapped his arms around me and pulled me in closer. Just having his arms wrapped around me made the world fade away.

Antonio grabbed the cold beer I set on the table and took a long swig. I could feel the tension in Antonio's body. He needed to tell me something, but he didn't want to.

A million bad things raced through my mind. Had Sophie been kidnapped or killed? Had Greg come after Lily again and actually got her? The longer the silence went on, the more I worried.

"Are you going to tell me what's wrong? The longer you're quiet, the more things I dream up."

He stiffened, took another swig of beer, then continued. "It's good and bad."

"Let's go to the living room and talk about this." Sitting on his lap in the dining room was not the most comfortable place to be having a conversation about anything bad. Antonio followed me into the living room.

Before I could sit down on the plush gray couch, Antonio pulled me onto his lap again. "Alex found Lily a job."

That was amazing. With everything Lily had been through, she deserved to find a job. "God, that's so amazing. I can't wait to celebrate with her."

Antonio's arms tightened around me. "Kitty..."

"Okay, tell me the bad news."

He huffed out a breath. "Alex looked for someone with good security. We wanted her to be safe wherever she went."

I waited for the shoe to drop.

After a pause, Antonio shook his head. "Have you heard of Jacob Black?"

Jacob Black owned Space Rock, one of the leaders in space exploration. He didn't just do businesses that dealt with space, though. He was one of the top innovators for clean energy. He was in the process of developing solar shingles that would power a house, which would no longer need regular electrical service. I nodded, letting Antonio continue.

He paused, and his voice came out strained. "I know you've become good friends with Lily, but I think this is a great opportunity for her. We can't let our feelings stand in the way."

"I'm confused, Antonio. Why do you think I would be upset about this?"

"Kitty Kat, Mr. Black runs his company out of Dallas. She will have to leave tomorrow, and you won't get to say goodbye. Greg is still out there, and we don't know when you can talk to her again."

I hadn't thought about that. Tears burned my eyes. Lily was the first true friend I'd found on my own. I wouldn't get to say goodbye, and I didn't know when I could see her again.

"Do you think Alex can find her something else?" I was being selfish. If I were her true friend, I would be happy for her.

Antonio let out a sigh and tightened his arms around me. I was already pressed tightly against his powerful chest. We sat there in silence.

"You know she needs to take this. Lily will be working directly with Mr. Black, and he promised to have at least two bodyguards on her and one on Tommy. Deep down, you know this is best for her even though it hurts you. I will keep looking for Greg, and once he is back behind bars or in one of your alligators' stomachs, you can jump on a plane and go see her."

I let out a huff. "You moved my alligators."

Antonio let out a chuckle. "When I know you've stopped killing people for sure, I will take you to visit them."

That put a smile on my face. I had grown to like my green monsters in the backyard.

I needed to think about what was best for my friend and not what I wanted. After being apart from people for so long, I wanted to collect them and keep them close, even though that made me sound like a serial killer. "Thank you," I said softly. It was a loaded thank you.

Antonio understood. He kissed the top of my head, and we sat in silence for couple of minutes. I leaned my head back and enjoyed his arms wrapped around my body.

Antonio grabbed his beer from the end table and took the last swig. "Where's my mini clone?"

"Your mom came by earlier and picked him up for the weekend."

"We have the house to ourselves all weekend?" The growl in Antonio's voice gave me tingles. "I can have my wicked way with my wife all weekend?"

The question he rumbled made my mouth go dry with anticipation.

I spun in Antonio's arms so that I straddled his waist and whispered in his ear, "You can have your wicked way with me anytime." I was rewarded with a groan.

"I can't wait to strip you naked."

I swallowed hard and tried to keep my body in control. I felt the desire run through me.

His lip curled into a smile. Antonio knew what he did to my body.

He reached up and tugged on a piece of hair that had fallen out of my messy bun. "Don't worry, Kitty Kat. I plan to have my wicked way with you all night. But I think we should have dinner first."

I couldn't believe Antonio. My body was on fire with need, and he wanted to eat. How could he even think about food at a time like this?

I wanted him, and he wanted me. Antonio's pupils were dilated. He needed me as much as I needed him.

When I ground my hips against his thick member, he tightened his arms around me and lifted me into the air.

"Kitty Kat, you're playing with fire." Antonio started down the hall toward the kitchen. If it meant my husband ended up naked, I would play with fire every day.

"I'm not hungry."

He whispered in my ear. "I'm hungry, and my dinner is in my hands. I can't wait to feast on that pussy all night."

In answer, I wrapped my fingers in Antonio's hair and pulled his lips to mine. He stopped and pushed me up against the wall. We were both panting by the time Antonio pulled back. "I love you," he whispered across my lips.

By the time we made it to the kitchen, we had both clawed at each other's clothes. Before I could figure out what he had planned, he tugged my jeans down and set me on the kitchen counter. My bare ass sat against the cool countertops.

Antonio's wide shoulders pried my legs apart. He leaned his head down and took my bundle of nerves into his lips. Normally, Antonio took his time. But instead, he licked his two fingers and pushed them in immediately. My juices helped him slide in with ease.

"You taste so good, Kitty Kat."

I didn't have time to respond before he took a long lick over my nub. The sensation of his rough tongue made my body go weak. I used my hands to keep my body supported.

"Please." I didn't know what I begged for. I needed more of anything he could give. My body was about to explode from arousal. I felt so close to him. I rolled my hips with every thrust of his hand. Antonio leaned over me and caught my lips in a kiss right before I went over the edge. He captured my moan in his mouth.

He stood back and yanked his shirt over his head. I couldn't help but groan when I saw his naked chest. Then he reached down to unbutton his jeans, and my mouth watered with need. While he was distracted by his task, I jumped off the counter and dropped to my knees.

I pulled Antonio's jeans down the remainder of the way and took his hard length in my mouth.

"Kat," he whispered as I worked him farther down my throat.

While I worked him in and out of my mouth, I reached up and cupped his balls. Antonio leaned forward, rested one hand on the counter, and wrapped his other hand in my hair.

He tried to control the speed at which I took him down my throat.

"You feel so good." Antonio held my head in place. He groaned when I ran my hand over his balls. When he released my hair, he reached down and lifted me under the arms. Then he turned me so I was bent over the counter. When I heard him step away, I went to turn.

"Stay."

I laid my head back down on the counter. I heard

him open the fridge, and his footsteps walked back toward the counter. "Damn, you have a nice ass." He placed a wet finger on my star. We had never had anal, but the thought of it sent a shiver of desire through my body. To have that man meant he had to possess every inch of my body.

"This will be mine one day, but I have other plans tonight."

I heard the sound of the whipped cream can a second before I felt the cool touch of the cream. Antonio bent down and licked the cream from my pussy. The new position was too much for my body to take. I was so aroused that the first lick sent me over the edge. I could feel my juices and the whipped cream on my thighs. I was ready for him.

"Oh my god," I whimpered. I rocked back, and Antonio ran his tongue across my nub. I couldn't hold back the second orgasm.

Antonio lined himself up and wrapped one arm around my stomach. His other hand rested on my shoulder, and he thrust into me. We both groaned at the connection. I felt so close to Antonio when he was inside me. It was a connection I couldn't quite explain. Every time we were together, I fell for him even more.

I hadn't known it was possible to love someone as much as I loved Antonio.

After a pause, he leisurely worked his girth in and

out. I pushed back to take him deeper into my channel. He filled me and touched all the right places.

Antonio sped up his thrust, hitting my G-spot with each one. I could feel the climax building. It wouldn't be long before I was consumed. I clenched my channel.

"Come," Antonio whispered as he pinched my clit. We went over at the same time. Antonio and I stayed connected until we caught our breath.

On the counter sat a pint of ice cream. We dropped to the floor and ate the ice cream off each other.

14

ANTONIO

The overhead light shone down on the conference room table, and pictures of Juan's men were plastered around the table. A map marked the location of Wild Hounds Bar in South Miami.

"Did you let Director Westblack know our plan?" Asher asked.

I ran a frustrated hand through my hair and looked in Zane's direction.

Zane held both hands up in surrender. "Don't look at me. You're the boss. That's your call, not mine."

I glanced around the room then looked down at the pictures scattered on the table. All the men had rap sheets longer than most gangbangers. Director Westblack wanted to find the weapons that went missing, and I had no doubt in my mind that the men on the table had what he was looking for. Juan needed to be eliminated. Once that task was done, I would turn the men over to Westblack.

"No. Do any of you have an issue with that?" This mission was personal to Zane and me. If any of the men in the room didn't feel comfortable with this mission, I wouldn't hold it against them. But they had to make their decision soon. I glanced up at the clock and noticed we were a go in two hours. I knew the men around the table would have my back. But it was their choice.

Asher was the first to speak out. "Brother, you know I have your back. I understand this mission is personal for you and Zane. But family sticks together through thick and thin, and we are family." He followed his speech with an "Oohra." The rest of the team followed.

I sat down at the head of the table, feeling thankful for the men who worked for me. Zane looked exhausted. He needed more than just to protect his wife. He needed Juan caught to help his brother's agenda. Zack had put a huge task on Zane. He had to clean up the CIA and find Juan, who we'd learned had more ties than we expected. "Zane, maybe you should sit this one out and stay with Sophie."

He shook his head. "Sophie is being transported to your house as we speak." My muscles tensed under his declaration. I hadn't agreed to that.

Before he could tell me why he'd made such a huge decision, Brock spoke up. "I have two of my men picking up Sophie and taking her to your house. They are going to stand guard while we are on the mission. It will be easier to guard one house. Bridget, Sophie, Jessica, and Daisy are going to your house as well. This way if this"—he waved his hand at the table—"is a setup, we have the women under surveillance."

The idea was good, but I didn't like that they had kept me out of this decision. "Fine. I think we need more than two guards."

Neal clicked a few buttons on his computer, and my house and all of its rooms appeared on the screen. Kat was in the bedroom, dancing in her underwear.

"Turn that off now." I didn't want the men around the table to see my wife half naked.

Neal's smile stretched across his face. "I didn't expect to see your wife half naked," Neal replied. "However, I'm going to stay back and man the surveillance. I will watch your house, and if anything looks out of the ordinary, I will radio the FBI or the Fort Lauderdale police department. I will also have eyes on you. Thanks to Uncle Sam, I have a satellite that can see pennies on the ground. If you guys get in trouble, I will also call for backup."

My anger evaporated the more Neal spoke. "Fine.

But let me tell Kat to put some clothes on before you pull my house up again."

Asher huffed out a breath. "Now that my brother has had his hissy fit for the day, let's talk about the operation. The men Juan is using are highly trained. We need to be on our A game."

I glanced over the military record of Ragnor Lynx, one of Juan's men. Two Purple Hearts and one Distinguished Service Medal. How could someone so good turn evil? Greed. That was the only thing that would turn good soldiers to the dark side.

The clock's loud tick was a constant reminder that time was not on our side. I texted Kat and told her to put clothes on. When I said we had pulled up the cameras in the house, she sent a bunch of angry emojis my way. A few minutes later, I got a text stating she was dressed.

When I had the okay from Kat, Neal pulled the cameras up in the house. Kat stood by the kitchen counter with her face to the camera. She had her middle finger raised and a smile on her face. She took my breath away every time I looked at her. Whether she was angry or happy, she was pretty.

Last night, I had bent her over the island and fucked her from behind. By the end, we both collapsed to the floor and shared a pint of ice cream.

When she leaned across the counter to grab the

paper, she looked up at the camera and winked. Her thoughts were running down the same paths as mine. It was almost like we could read each other's minds.

Asher cleared his throat to get my attention. "If you're done ogling your wife, we have shit to do." I could hear a hint of laughter in his voice.

I peeled my eyes away from the screen and gave Asher my attention. "What did I miss?" I wasn't going to apologize for my actions.

Asher rolled his eyes. "I think we should have Jacob set up here with his sniper rifle." He pointed to a high-rise building a half mile away from the bar. The shot from there would be difficult for some, but Jacob was one of the best snipers, almost as good as my wife. "I think we should use Eric on the back of the building." Eric worked for Brock and Blackwood Security. He was another renowned sniper.

The plan made sense. Zane, Brock, Asher, and I would go to the meeting. "Is CJ heading over to my house?" I would feel better if he were with them. He worked behind a computer and had no military field training.

When CJ opened his mouth, Asher raised his eyebrows. "I would watch what you say next very carefully." CJ crossed his arms over his chest and sank back into the chair. He was not pleased with his Dom.

"Yes, CJ will be at your house. If the mission goes bad, I don't want him to watch."

I could tell from the look in CJ's eyes that he was going to watch anyway. Hell, I knew my wife would talk Sophie into hacking a computer so she could watch us take down Juan. "Thank you."

"Do you think Sophie and Kat will stay at the house?" Asher asked. "You know they both want to kill him for what he did to their family."

"Kat promised she wouldn't do anything stupid." The words didn't sound very convincing. "The only way we could guarantee they wouldn't come is if we locked them in a safe room. And that would be pointless because we know Sophie could break out of it. We have to have faith in them."

"Sophie thinks we are going in around ten. We should be done by the time they could sneak past the guards," Zane muttered.

I gave CJ a pointed look. "If we are going to keep our wives out of this. You can't tell them what time."

CJ nodded. His lips were pressed tightly together. He agreed with me but didn't look as if he liked it.

The time had ticked by quickly. It was time to gear up and head out. I had received a text from Kat that said Sophie had arrived. It was followed by more emojis I didn't understand. What the hell did an eggplant mean?

"It's go time," I informed the room. Everyone started to file out and head to the armory next to the conference room.

We would be going on the mission in full tactical gear. I wouldn't lose any of my men to these terrorists.

I grabbed CJ by the arm before he walked out. "CJ, take vests for you and the girls." CJ understood how dangerous the mission was. He didn't protest and headed toward the armory with the rest of the men.

In my office, I pulled a bulletproof vest over my head. After everything was in place, I put on a second black T-shirt to cover up the vest. I grabbed my Glock off the desk and put it in my side holster and pulled out another Glock from my desk drawer and attached it to my ankle. To make sure I was fully loaded, I grabbed my MK3 military knife and attached it to my other ankle. The knock on the door had me look up.

"You ready, brother?"

"Yes." I gazed past Asher into the reception area, where the team had gathered.

The drive from AA Security to South Miami would take an hour. I headed out the door toward the SUVs. They had been packed with extra ammo and guns. The footsteps behind me let me know the men were following.

Brock and his team got into one SUV, and our team

occupied the other. The SUV hummed with energy. The adrenaline before a fight was high.

Asher was the first to break the silence. "Are we bringing Juan in, or are we going to take him out?"

I caught Zane's eyes in the mirror and saw a mix of emotions pass through them.

"If we can bring him in alive, we do. Under no circumstances do we kill on first sight." If we took Juan out when he was unarmed, we'd be no better than he was.

"I agree. Don't get me wrong—I want him dead, and I worry he still has friends in places we haven't found, and they might help him escape," Zane gritted through his teeth.

An hour later, we made it to our stop. We parked three buildings down from the bar and hoofed it until we had a plain-sight view of the front of the bar. I reached up and pressed the com in my ear. "Eric, are you in place?"

"Yes, sir. I have a clear view of the back entrance. No movement at the moment."

"Jacob?"

"You're in my sights, boss. I see a black town car three blocks away, approaching from the east."

This was it, the day we would put Juan behind us, and I could spend the rest of my life spoiling my wife and keeping her out of trouble.

Before the town car appeared, three men stepped out of the bar. They looked around at their surroundings. I pulled out a pair of binoculars to get a better look. When their faces came into focus, I recognized them from the photo. They were Juan's team.

The black town car pulled into the parking lot, and the back door swung open. Two men stepped out of the car. I thought our mission was blown until Juan finally stepped out last.

15

KAT

As I took a sip of the crisp white wine in my hand, I couldn't help but think it wasn't strong enough to deal with the situation at hand. I wanted to be out in the field and take the shot that ended Juan's life. But Antonio's lecture about why I needed to stay back played through my head.

The little boy on the floor playing with his baby cousin was the reason I was here. I would do anything to protect my son. No one could do that better than me.

Rain started to patter on the outside of the house. In Florida, it could rain on one side of the street and not the other. I hoped it was clear where Antonio and his team had headed to take down Juan. Rain would add an extra layer of difficulty to the operation.

"Can you pull up the radar?" I asked CJ, who was

glued to his laptop. "Find out if it's raining in South Miami."

CJ didn't look up from his laptop. "It's not raining there at the moment, but the clouds are rolling in." His body was tense as he spoke.

I wouldn't ask to see his screen, period. I had faith in Antonio. He would call the second the operation was over.

Bridget picked up her wine glass filled with grape juice and heaved a sigh of frustration at the nonalcoholic drink. She proceeded to plop down on the brown recliner so she could elevate her feet. When the footstool popped out, she groaned in relief. Bridget was in her eighth month, and she told us every day how her feet and back hurt. A memory from my pregnancy floated through my mind. When I was eight months pregnant and Ant continued to kick my ribs at night, I would get up, rub my stomach, and talk about his father. He would settle at the sound of my voice or the stories I told.

Cross-legged on the couch, Sophie leaned over the side to peek at CJ's screen. "Watching that will make you go crazy. Why don't you put it down?" When CJ gave her a strange look Sophie continued, "Don't act like the raid isn't going on. Kat has Antonio's office bugged. Also, the quick change of the screens every time I lean over is a further giveaway."

For the first time, CJ's eyes left the computer screen and narrowed in Sophie's direction. "I don't understand how both of you are not worried and wanting to see what's going on. Last time, you took things into your own hands."

I reached for the remote to start some music. My nineties playlist played in the background, drowning out the sound of rain hitting the house.

It took a minute for me to gather my thoughts enough to answer CJ's question. It *was* hard for me to sit back and wait.

"You're right. God, I want to be there and take the kill shot. For what Juan did to our family, I want to watch the life drain from him. But last time, I froze and let him get away. I don't think I would freeze again, but what if I did, and someone didn't arrive in time to save me?"

Sophie played with the glass in her hands for a second. "Why did you freeze?"

Fuck. I never talked to her about this after it happened. Antonio and I had talked about it a few times, and he understood. Would Sophie understand, or would she be hurt? I let out the breath I held.

"He raised me." I held up my hand to stop her before she spoke. "I know he was a horrible guardian, but he was all I knew for most of my life, and I paused."

Sophie frowned. "I can see that. He was an ass to

me for years, but no matter how many times I say I could kill him, I'm not sure I could pull the trigger."

Bridget worked to change the subject, and I appreciated her for doing so. "Are you guys going to Neal's house for Christmas this year?"

Patty and Sam were coming home for Christmas. I was excited to meet Jessica's sister.

"I can't wait to see my nephew," Jessica said. She had told us she hadn't been back since Patty delivered but was planning on going to the wedding next March. Jessica had been captured and tortured twice in her home country. The men who almost killed her were all dead, but she still had anxiety about her home country.

Daisy spoke up for the first time. She had been sitting on the floor with the kids, listening to the conversation. "Daisy and Neal invited too many people, so we're moving it to Club Sanctorum."

"Did you invite Aaron?" Aaron was Antonio and Asher's younger brother. He looked like he had a thing for Daisy at the Ross family get together. Daisy was currently Neal's sub, and Neal hadn't looked happy when Aaron had given her a hug. I couldn't wait to see what happened.

A light blush came over Daisy's face. "Daisy invited Aaron." She picked up Alex Jr. before continuing. "Aaron used to be one of Daisy's Doms, and he treated Daisy well. Neal is okay with Aaron coming but he told Aaron Daisy was his."

CJ barked out a laugh. "Neal threatened to cut Aaron's dick off if he ever touched you again."

"Daisy didn't know Neal said that. Aaron has a nice dick. It would be a waste if Neal cut it off."

Everyone in the room burst out laughing. The wine in my mouth flew everywhere. Daisy tried to keep a straight face, as though she didn't understand what she'd said, but she lost it like everyone else in the room.

This was what I had missed by going years with no friends. But no matter how much I laughed with the people around me, I was still worried about Antonio. My head and heart were focused on Antonio and his mission. A wave of unease rushed through my body.

"I can't wait to see what happens next time you and Neal are at Club Sanctorum and Aaron shows up," CJ said.

A smile lit Daisy face. "Hopefully a three—"

Glass shattered in the kitchen, and everyone's eyes turned toward the noise. Muffled voices drowned out the sound of rain. I jumped up and grabbed Ant and Alex Jr. in my hands and ran down the hall to the panic room. Getting the boys to a safe place was my number-one concern.

I could hear shouts from the kitchen. The lock mechanism opened when I pressed my thumb to the pad, and the steel-reinforced door opened. Tears ran down Ant's chubby cheeks. I set him and his cousin in the room and put a finger to my lips for them to be quiet. "Take care of your cousin. I will be back soon."

The door closed with a thud. I could hear faint cries from the other side. My heart broke when I stepped away from the door. I wanted to turn back and cradle my baby in my arms. Instead, I had to deal with someone who thought they could break into my house.

I reached for my phone to dial 9-1-1, but cell service had been disrupted. I couldn't send a text out or let anyone know we needed help. The room next to the panic room was Antonio's office. In the safe, he kept a large supply of weapons. After I input the date of our wedding, the safe popped open, and I grabbed two Glocks and shut the safe door.

I could hear Bridget's cries in the hall. "Who—" Bridget asked before a loud sound of skin hitting skin echoed through the house and cut off her words.

"Where is the redhead?" The men wanted me. When I peeked around the corner, three men's faces came into view—Juan's men. Had Antonio been sent into a trap?

All three men were heavily armed.

Adrenaline coursed through my veins.

Sophie growled when one of the men pointed his guns at Bridget's belly.

I raised the gun in my hand and walked around the corner. My heart was kicking against my ribs. I wasn't going to let anybody come into my house and harm my family.

"What do you want?" I spotted a fourth man in the kitchen. *Damn.* When my gaze went past him, I saw Brock's two men lying on the ground outside the door. My gut twisted, thinking they might be dead.

The gunman's eyes focused on me. In my peripheral vision, I saw Sophie reach under the table. Antonio was like Zane in that he had guns under the coffee tables. Ours also had to have a thumbprint for release. Antonio had uploaded all our friends' prints in case this very situation occurred.

I saw Bridget reach for her phone and swipe her finger across it. She was trying to dial 9-1-1. She didn't know they had jammed the cell frequency. Her call wouldn't go out.

To keep the men's attention from my friends in the room, I walked to the right and headed for the kitchen. "What do you guys want? Did Juan send you?" I asked a second time. I tried to keep my voice calm.

The only hope we had was that Neal's cameras were on and he would send help. Four gunmen would be a hard fight.

Fear fought to take over. My friends and family were in danger.

The thug who seemed to be the leader stepped forward. He was the biggest of the men. His bulky body was three times my size. "Where is the ledger, you cunt?" he snarled at me.

Ledger? What ledger did they want? I was about to respond when it hit me. *Fuck.* The ledger I took from the bunker. When I got home from being detained, I placed it in a kitchen drawer. With everything that happened, I forgot about it.

When I didn't respond right away, he motioned to one of his men, who moved his gun from me to Sophie. I forced myself to keep my cool. If I showed any type of vulnerability, they would take action.

"It's in the kitchen. Follow me." I hoped someone in the living room could use this moment to strike.

"Don't be dumb, bitch. Tell me where it is, and I will get it."

I pointed toward the kitchen drawer.

When the leader turned to walk past me, I used the opportunity to hit him over the head with the butt of the gun. He dropped to the floor with a thud.

"You fucking bi—" a man almost as large as the leader shouted. He swiveled his gun in my direction. Before he had time to fire, a loud bang sounded from Daisy's direction.

She was standing, with her eyes level with the target she had taken out. Her cheerful smile was gone.

With my attention on Daisy, I didn't hear the leader get up from the ground. A thick arm came around my throat. "Drop the gun, or this bitch dies."

With my eyes, I pleaded with Daisy not to listen, but she obeyed and lowered the gun to the floor. Bridget had tears streaming down her face.

A glint of silver in Sophie's direction caught my eye. She had a gun.

"Boss, we need to hurry up."

The leader had dragged me over to the kitchen island. "Open it."

I slid the drawer open and pulled out the brown leather ledger. The leader grunted in approval.

"We got what we needed, men. Let's kill them and head out."

The sound of Bridget's scream broke my heart. It was one of the last things I remembered before the sound of a gun and then the sheer pain in my side. "I love you, Antonio," I whispered before the world went dark.

16

ANTONIO

Juan and his men had entered the dilapidated bar five minutes ago. A neon light hung on the side of the bar flashed "Wild Hounds," half of the letters burnt out.

The red paint on the building had lost its shine. What used to be a window next to the front door was boarded up with a piece of plywood. The sound of broken glass crunched under my boots with each step across the parking lot.

I didn't need to look to my right to know Zane was in step with me. Over the past couple months, we had become synced with each other.

In the back, I could see the Florida sun setting over the building. It was in direct contrast to our location. The impending night was a reminder we needed to hurry this along before the bar opened. I glanced down at my watch and calculated how much time we had. In one hour, the bar patrons would start to arrive.

"I have eyes and audio inside," came Neal's voice over the com.

"Brock, are you in place?" Brock and his employee John took the back door.

Neal gave us an update. Juan seemed to be in an argument with his men. He was under the impression they had captured Sophie and Kat. Neal checked the feed to my house and informed me Kat and Sophie were fine.

I had second-guessed myself all day about Kat being on this op. She was one of the best sharpshooters we had. But if she were here, it would distract me. When Kat had agreed to stay with Ant while Zane and I worked the op, I worried she would find a way here. Yet Neal had confirmed that she didn't leave the house. Knowing Kat was still safe settled me.

"They look distracted. Time to move in," Neal's voice echoed in my ear.

The remaining members of the team checked in. They were good to go.

I reached for the door handle. Wild Hound's door opened with no resistance. When the door had cracked the first inch, I could hear Juan's raised voice.

Everyone in the room seemed to be distracted by Juan. Zane and I entered the room and stood to watch the scene in front of us. The smell of cheap whiskey and stale cigarettes hit me like a ton of bricks. The inside of the bar was not much better than the outside. Dirt and empty bottles lined the floor. I could see one chair that was broken. The tables leaned to the side and still had the bottles from last night on them. Behind the bar, only a few cheap bottles of liquor sat. It took a good two minutes before one of Juan's men saw us by the front door.

"Good afternoon, Uncle. I think it's time we had a chat."

Juan's face turned red with anger when his eyes landed on Zane and me. He didn't respond to my statement. Juan swung his head back at his men and narrowed his beady eyes. "You sent me photos of those two dead. I will have you fucking killed if you don't eliminate them."

"Such a temper, Uncle. Let's sit down and have a little chat. You can clearly see Zane and I aren't dead."

Juan balled his fists. "Stop calling me Uncle."

I looked over at Brock and John, who held back their grins. Even before Juan had destroyed my life, I hated the man. "Well, I am married to your niece, Uncle."

Juan sat down at the table and motioned for me to join him. Weiss was the leader of the three in the room. His jaw was clenched, and he took the table next to ours. Brock stayed in the back of the room while John worked himself around to get another angle if things went down.

Zane and I took our seats at the table across from Juan. My hand never left my Glock. The only people I trusted in the room were the men that came with me. We waited at the table for Juan to say something. My goal was for him to tell us what he wanted, and when we had the upper hand, we would take him down.

"I want all the money back, and your plane."

I tapped my finger on the table. "Let me get this straight. You want Sophie's and Katherine's inheritance and my plane?"

Juan's hand trembled slightly. It was the first time I had seen him not completely composed. His three men looked to be in a heated discussion at the other table. Brock had his full attention on them, and John stood as our backup.

"It was my money. Those dumb bitches had no right to my inheritance." He jumped from his seat and started to pace back and forth. "It was my money. It was my money."

His rant kept on. It seemed that Juan had had a breakdown. When I looked closer, his usually perfectly groomed hair was greasy and unkempt. His thousand-dollar suit was riddled with dirt, and the bags under his eyes were almost black.

Weiss was the commander of his unit. Did something happen that we were not prepared for? He narrowed his eyes in Juan's direction and stood up from his chair.

"Shut the fuck up." He raised his gun at Juan and pulled the trigger twice. It was a perfect double tap.

I glanced in Zane's direction for a second to see his reaction. His eyes zeroed in on Weiss. Brock's eyes were wide in surprise. John was to my back.

Neal's voice came over the com. "That was unexpected. Time to roll, guys. Three blocks down, tonight's patrons are approaching your way."

"How many?" I whispered into the com.

"Looks to be around fifteen."

An audible curse came from Zane's direction. Those weren't bar patrons on their way to get a drink. Those were Weiss's backup for whatever he had planned. This was a setup.

I stood up from the wooden chair. "Since you've eliminated the only person we care about, we'll be on our way." I didn't have any issue with Weiss and his men, but when I got out of there, I would call Director Westblack and let him know where he could find the men who stole the guns.

Zane and I started to back toward the door. Out of the corner of my eye, I caught a glimpse of Brock and John moving toward the back door.

"Don't take another fuckin' step." When Brock and John continued back, Weiss shot his gun at the ceiling. At the moment, we had them outnumbered. Only two of his men stood with him. The odds were not in their favor.

I kept my grip on my sidearm. "Weiss, we have no beef with you."

"I don't give a shit about you. If you take one more step, you will look like him." He pointed to Juan's body. "If your wife would've left things alone, we wouldn't be here now."

Fuck. What had Kat done to piss these men off? We had shared all the evidence with each other, but nothing came to mind that would explain why she would have made them angry. When I went to ask Neal to see what he could find, the com in my ear screeched. The com frequency had been jammed.

I heard the rumble of motorcycles approach the building. Whatever was on the other side of the door would be worse if we left the three men inside alive. I didn't wait. I raised the Glock in my hand and repeated what Weiss did earlier. Zane did the same to the man that had stood next to Weiss. They both dropped to the ground with perfect holes in their heads, and Brock took the last man down.

The device killing the com frequency had to be in one of the men's pockets. I ran toward the bodies and started to search. Zane understood what I needed to find and joined me. The last body we searched had the device on it. I flipped the switch over, and Neal's voice came across.

"Can you hear me?"

"Yes. Sitrep."

Neal's voice wasn't the next to come across the com. It was Jacob's. "You have incoming. Ten entering the front of the bar and five at the back."

It was going to be a bloodbath if we didn't get backup ourselves. Zane and I positioned ourselves behind the bar. John and Brock overturned a couple tables and took cover behind them.

Director Westblack's voice came over the com. "Antonio, you want to tell me why the fuck you are in the middle of a shootout, and I wasn't informed about the operation before you went?"

Neal must've called Westblack when the com and video feeds went down. "It's classified. We could use a little help if you have men in the area."

I heard Westblack grumble, "Classified my ass. We are five minutes out. Try not to kill everyone. We need information."

Before I had time to respond, the door to the bar flung open and cracked against the wall. The first man to step through the door was close to seven feet tall and dressed in leather pants and a leather jacket. The scar down the side of his face gave the man a heightened sense of menace.

A group of bikers followed him in, and the small bar became overcrowded. The scarred biker was the first to speak. "Who killed Weiss?"

"We have no issue with you. Juan was our target. Let us go, and we won't have any more issues." With each word I spoke, the biker leader snarled with anger.

He worked his way across the bar, throwing tables out of the way to make a path to the bar. His men followed behind them. They were so concentrated on Zane and me that they ignored Brock and John behind them. Brock and John slowly crept their way up behind the group of men.

Zane and I needed to keep the men looking our way so Brock and John could take them out one at a time from behind. "Two minutes," Westblack echoed through my ear.

Neal's voice came back over the com at the same time the leader put his hands on the bar. Neal said, "Someone breached your house. You guys need to get out of there and head to Antonio's. I called the police."

This was the play all along—to get my wife by herself and us unable to get to her. What information did Kat have? The leader had said something I didn't catch because my head was on Kat.

"We do things differently in Wild Hounds," one of

the bikers was saying. "An eye for an eye. You"—he pointed at me—"killed three of my friends. Now you get to decide which three of yours are goi—"

His words were cut off when FBI agents swarmed the building. Within seconds, the bikers were on the floor and detained.

I passed Westblack on my way out the door. "Brock is still in there and will help you with everything you need. You need to call the president and tell him Juan is dead. The rest of the group is going after my wife."

Zane and I were running for the SUV. "Neal, tell me what's going on."

"The feed was cut. I can't see anything. The police are ten minutes out."

Zane slammed his hands against the dash and let out a string of cuss words. "I can't lose Sophie. She's my world."

"Don't worry. They will be fine." I didn't believe the words I spoke.

17
───────
ANTONIO

I gripped the passenger door while Zane weaved through traffic on our way back to my house. The cabin was filled with tension. The Wild Hounds bar was a half hour from my house. A red car swerved in front of our SUV, and Zane slammed on the brakes. He was quick to move to the other lane and slammed his foot back down so the SUV lurched forward.

My heart beat so fast that I felt like it was about to jump out of my chest. When I glanced in the rearview mirror, I saw Asher and Brock on our bumper. Neal had left his post at the command center and headed toward my house. Everyone we loved was in that house.

We were halfway there when I heard the beep of Zane's phone. I reached for it so he could concentrate on the road. It was a text from Sophie.

I'm safe honey, but please hurry home.

While I read Sophie's text, Asher and Neal both spoke through the com and stated they had heard from their loved ones.

I reached for my phone, but no message appeared. I texted Kat and asked if she was okay. No response. My hands shook as I typed each letter in Zane's phone to Sophie. *Tell Kat to text Antonio.* Bubbles appeared as if she was typing and then went away. I waited two minutes, but no text came through.

I called Kat's phone, and nobody answered. I tried Sophie's phone, and she sent me to voicemail. *Fuck.* I was going to lose her again. "Why the fuck are they not answering? Asher, call CJ and ask if Kat and Ant are okay," I demanded through the com.

He responded that he would try. The time on the dashboard clock slowly ticked by.

Zane glanced my way for a second. "Stop that train of thought. Kat is tough. She can make it through anything. Let's get to the house and see what happened."

It felt like it took Asher hours to respond. His voice was low and filled with worry. "Ant is fine. Your parents just showed up. Neal is also at the scene." There was a long pause. I didn't think he would tell me about my wife. "Kat is alive."

Alive. What the fuck did that mean. "Tell someone to make her call me."

"She can't call you at the moment."

The last ten minutes to the house felt like hours. Nobody would tell me if Kitty Kat had been hurt. Zane pulled around the last corner. My house sat at the end of the street. Blue and red lights beamed to a point that it was hard to see the road.

Zane hadn't even put the SUV in park by the time I jumped out the passenger door. My boots hit the cement, and I ran down the street at full speed toward the house. When I went to duck under the yellow police tape, an officer tried to stop me.

"You can't go over there, sir."

I pushed him to the side. "That's my fucking house."

He grabbed my arm and tried to drag me back.

"So help me, if you don't take your hands off m—"

My words were cut off by Detective Higgins before I could threaten the police officer.

"Let him go, Officer Carl. Antonio, settle down, and I will take you to your wife."

I saw a stretcher being wheeled out from the entryway of my house. Kat's red hair hung over the edge. I didn't hear anything else around me. I ran toward my wife.

When I reached Kat's side, her eyes were closed,

and blood marred her beautiful face. I gripped her hand and brought it to my face. Her hand was warm, and I felt her squeeze when I whispered her name. Someone kept trying to pull me away from Kat. I felt the wetness drip down my face.

"Sir, you need to move. We are trying to help her." I stepped back so the paramedics could work on her. I glanced around the front yard to find my boy. He was in my mom's arms. I was torn between the need to hug Ant to make sure he was okay and the need to follow the men who carted my wife away.

Sophie rested her hand on my back. "Let Zane and I drive you to the hospital, and Ant can ride with us. The paramedics will need to work on Kat."

When I turned to see Kat again, the ambulance had closed the door and taken off. Shouts came from the front doorway of the house. The cops escorted three men out the front of the house, all in handcuffs, followed by another body on a stretcher.

I walked over to my mom and grabbed Ant out of her arms. He laid his head on my shoulder. I didn't say a word as I walked toward Zane's SUV.

"Mommy's going to be okay," Ant whispered in my ear.

I squeezed him to my chest. "I know, son."

But I didn't. Kat looked lifeless on the stretcher. If she hadn't squeezed my hand, I would have thought she was gone. The only sound in the car to the hospital was Sophie's sniffles from the front seat.

WHEN WE ARRIVED at the hospital, we were directed to the waiting room. Kat was rushed into surgery. A bullet had hit Kat's pelvic bone and traveled upward. The last we heard was that they didn't know what damage had been done. They were concerned because when Kat had been shot, she had fallen backward, and her head hit the corner of the countertop.

Everyone had made it to the hospital. Brock and Jessica were the last to show. They stayed at my house until FBI Director Westblack arrived. Brock handed the leather ledger over to the FBI. I was still shocked she had kept that in a kitchen drawer. Westblack had said he would let us know what he found out.

Daisy had withdrawn into herself since we arrived at the hospital. She blamed herself for Kat being shot. She thought if she would've kept the gun in her hand, Kat wouldn't have been shot. But these men were ruthless, and Daisy would've been killed if she hadn't dropped the gun when she did.

When the police arrived, they heard the gunshot and rushed the house. They were able to get Kat medical attention immediately. If Neal hadn't called the police the second he noticed something go wrong, Kat would be dead.

Alex and Bridget stopped by the emergency room to make sure Bridget and the baby were okay. Bridget's right eye had started to blacken from when one of the men hit her.

My parents took Ant and Alex Jr. back to their house. The hospital waiting room was not a place for Ant to be, but it had been hard for me to release him.

I took a sip of the hospital coffee. It tasted more like motor oil. "Sophie, you and Zane can head home. I will call you as soon as I hear something."

Sophie shifted in Zane's lap and narrowed her eyes. "That is my sister back there." She pointed toward the white double doors. "I'm not going anywhere until I see her."

When I looked in CJ and Asher's direction. CJ's fingers were typing across the laptop. He hadn't put it down since we had arrived. "Don't even say it, Antonio. We are not leaving."

"Nobody has eaten for the past few hours. We went from an OP to the emergency room. Why don't you get something to eat?"

Nobody moved.

Asher leaned back in his chair. "Jacob is bringing everyone food."

Next to Neal, Daisy continued to cry. I walked over to where they sat.

"Can I sit next to you, Daisy?"

She nodded a watery smile at me.

"You know, Kat would be proud of you for the shot you took earlier. I bet when she wakes up, it will be one of the first things she talks about. Sophie told me on the way over that she was amazed with your aim and poise."

"Daisy was kidnapped for years. Now, Daisy goes to the shooting range once a week for target practice." Neal's jaw twitched at her admission. I raised my eyebrow, and he shook his head. I would ask him what his problem was later.

I reached over and grabbed Daisy's chin, ignoring the growl from Neal's direction. "Kat is a fighter. She will be fine. When she gets out, I bet she will go to the shooting range with you."

"Daisy would like that."

Jacob showed up with tacos for everyone in the waiting room. For the next half hour, we told stories about Kat. Women from the outreach center called and left messages on Kat's phone. She received many texts from the women. I had left a message with the center saying Kat wouldn't be in. I hadn't anticipated the response we received. Kat was loved at the center. Everyone that met Kat couldn't help but fall in love.

She had been in surgery for six hours. When I stood to stretch my back, the double white doors opened.

A doctor in his late fifties stood with a clipboard in his hand. Next to him stood a blond nurse. They both had serious looks on their face. I rushed toward them.

"Mr. Ross?" the male doctor asked.

"Yes. Can I see Kat?"

The doctor let out a sigh. "How about we go talk in a room?"

Kat's family and friends were all around me. Anything the doctor had to say could be said in front of our family. "We can talk here. Is my wife okay."

He eyed me for a second. "Kat is out of surgery and in recovery. Her recovery is going to be long and hard. We had to remove her gallbladder and part of her liver. The bullet hit her pelvic bone and traveled upward. It did a lot of damage on its path. She will be fine in a few months. Until then, she will need to rest."

"I want to see her now."

"Kat will be out for a while, maybe days. She hit her head hard. Go home, take a shower, and have a night's rest."

I thought the doctor had better let me see my wife or I would knock his ass down and look in every room until I found her.

"I don't care. I want to see her now."

He finally nodded at the nurse next to him. I grabbed Sophie's hand and followed the nurse. I knew she wanted to see her sister as badly as I needed to see Kat.

The nurse opened the door to Kat's room. The sight in front of me hit me like a freight train. Kat had a white gauze bandaged wrapped around her head. The machines made the only noise in the room. Sophie rushed to Kat's side, grabbed her hand, and cried.

I took Kat's other side and couldn't hold back the tears. I had almost lost my wife a second time.

KAT

I had been in the hospital for four days. Antonio hadn't left my room. The farthest he'd gone was to the bathroom. I loved my husband to death, but he needed to go home, shower, and have a good night's sleep.

Juan and his men were in jail or dead. We didn't have anything to worry about anymore. Antonio and I had talked about that night, and we each had different parts that scared us. My heart still pounded when I thought about someone breaking into our house with Ant home. He could have been hurt. Antonio had had to see my almost-lifeless body.

"Honey, go home tonight. Jacob will be right outside the door. No one will come after me."

Antonio shifted in his chair. "I'm fine where I am."

Jesus, I was married to the most stubborn man alive. "I need you to go home and grab me some clothes to wear out of the hospital tomorrow. While you're there, take a shower and a nap." When it looked like he was about to argue again, I begged. "Please. I've worn the plaid hospital nightgown long enough. I don't want to wear any hospital clothes home."

"Fine." Antonio leaned down and brushed his lips against mine before he left the room.

I reached for my phone to work on my missed messages. Each day, they piled up. I had a missed text from Sophie. Attached to the message was a picture of FBI Director Westblack standing next to crates of military-grade weapons.

When I went to click on the link, my stomach growled.

I texted Jacob, who stood guard outside my room.

Can u get me something to eat?

I heard the ding on his phone, and his reply came back immediately.

I can't leave. I will have Antonio grab you something.

"No!" I yelled from my room. Jacob appeared in the doorway.

"Please run down to the café and get me a sandwich. Nobody will kidnap me in five minutes."

He looked at his phone and typed out a message.

Someone approached Jacob from behind. He was so quick I didn't have time to yell for Jacob to turn. The masked man drove a needle into Jacobs neck and pulled his limp body into my hospital room. With the door closed the intruder dropped Jacob to the ground and put a hand over my mouth before I could scream.

"Where is she?"

The intruder was dressed in blue scrubs and a white jacket to match. He had a mask over his face, but I recognized his voice and beady eyes. Greg stood above my bed. I moved my hand to the side to click the call button. Greg lurched and grabbed it before I could. He leaned into me and pressed his hand on my side where the stitches were still fresh.

The pain that shot through my body was enough to make my vision sway. But I wouldn't let him win. He would never get to Lily. I scratched my arm to pull my IV out. When it ripped out of my skin, I held it in my hand. Greg was within arm's reach. I used what energy I had to force my arm forward and jabbed the needle into his neck.

Greg's scream hurt my ears. It was so loud that it could be heard from the nurses' station. Greg ripped the needle out of his neck and held one hand to the hole that squirted blood. He balled up his other fist. I didn't have anything else to protect myself with, so I covered my head and waited for the first blow to come.

It never came. Instead, I heard a grunt and a thud on the ground. Antonio stood over Greg, who lay on the floor in the fetal position. Hospital security came into the room.

"He tried to kill my wife and took out one of my agents. Call Detective Higgins at the police department. He knows this man has made a few attempts. This one should put him away for good." When the officers turned for a second, Antonio kicked Greg in the side. The man started to cry.

A team of nurses rushed to Jacob's side. A half hour later Doctor O'Malley let Antonio know Jacob would be okay. He was given a high dose of sedatives.

The hospital police escorted Greg out of the room. For the next hour, they cleaned up the wound in my arm from where I pulled out my IV. Antonio was very quiet the whole time.

Once everyone had left, I patted the edge of my bed and scooted over to the side. Antonio didn't waste a second before he climbed in next to me.

"I thought you were going home."

"Jacob texted that you needed food. I grabbed you something and headed back up."

For once, I was glad Antonio had been overprotective. The sedative Greg gave Jacob knocked him out for a few hours. When he woke up he was pissed and wanted to kill Greg. He also felt guilty for Greg's attack. But with Greg and Juan both out of the picture, we could finally move on with our lives. I wasn't upset with Jacob. For once I was happy he contacted Antonio and asked him to grab my food.

"Thanks for being my hero."

"I would do anything for you." Antonio wrapped an arm around me and kissed my forehead.

"I love you."

EPILOGUE

Antonio

Ant's birthday party was in full swing. Kat's idea for a detective party was a hit. We came up with two cases. When they solved the first case, the kids received half of the gear for laser tag. The second case led them to the rest of the gear. For the past hour, Ant and his friends had run around the yard. Kat and I had rented equipment for the adults too. Once the kids went inside to watch a movie, the game would be on. We planned to play women against men.

Kat walked toward me, her white summer dress blowing in the Florida breeze. She still favored her right side, even though it had been two months since she was shot.

She wrapped her arms around me. "His birthday is perfect. Thank you, Antonio."

I leaned down and kissed the top of her head. "I didn't do anything. You put this all together. Have I told you how amazing a mom you are today?"

Kat giggled. "You tell me every five seconds, but I love to hear you say it."

We sat in the chairs on the back porch, and I gazed across the backyard. I was lucky to have so many friends and family. With Kat by my side, my life was almost perfect. I laid my hand on her belly. This week we had made a quick trip to the doctor. Kat had suffered nausea for the past week.

The doctor confirmed our suspicion that Kat was seven weeks pregnant with twins. I wanted to shout the news from the rooftops, but Kat wanted us to wait for the three-month mark. I would do anything she asked.

Neal and Daisy took two open chairs. Neal leaned back in his chair and grabbed Daisy's hand.

"My brother Aaron texted this morning to tell me he was on his way back from Los Angeles."

Neal grumbled something under his breath. Daisy playfully tapped him on the shoulder. "Neal is going to take Daisy to Los Angeles in two weeks. Daisy hasn't been back since she was kidnapped. Daisy is excited and worried."

Neal pinched the bridge of his nose. "You don't happen to have an extra bodyguard, do you?"

"Jacob can go with you."

At that same moment, Jacob stepped onto the patio. "Go where?"

"Neal and Daisy need a bodyguard for their trip to Los Angeles in a couple weeks."

Jacob nodded and took a swig of his beer.

Asher and CJ were the next to join us on the patio. "When is the due date?" Asher asked.

I looked at Kat. "You told him?"

Kat went to pull her hand away, but I gripped it harder so she couldn't move. "No. How did you figure it out?"

"It wasn't hard. You both have been glowing all day. Yesterday, Antonio was in a panic because you had been sick for too many days and he was worried about you."

A smile spread across my wife's face. She was more beautiful each day. "I'm seven weeks. We were going to wait to tell everyone until the three-month mark, but we are having twins."

Our group of friends gave us hugs and well wishes.

My phone vibrated with an incoming text from Detective Higgins.

Greg's case is scheduled for next week.

That would be something to worry about tomorrow. Today, I would enjoy the friends around me.

"I love you, Kitty Kat."

THE END

CLICK HERE TO JOIN MY NEWSLETTER!
JOIN MY FACEBOOK GROUP FOR LATEST BOOK INFO!

AUTHOR'S NOTE

White Hat Security Series

Hacker Exposed
Royal Hacker
Misunderstood Hacker
Undercover Hacker
Hacker Revelation

Montana Gold (Brotherhood Kindle World)

Grayson's Angel
Noah - Oct 23, 2018

A Flipping Love Story (Badge of Honor World)

Unlocking Dreams - Nov 13, 2018
Unlocking Hope - 2019

Visit linzibaxter.com for more information and release dates.
Join Linzi Baxter Newsletter at Newsletter

GRAYSON'S ANGEL
MONTANA GOLD

A life she thought she left behind...

Kara Davidson left Montana years ago. After her mother died, she decided to never step foot in the state again. Then she gets a call saying her father is in the hospital. Her trip home is supposed to be quick. She didn't count on meeting a retired Navy SEAL who made her body come alive.

A retired Navy SEAL looking forward to vacation...

Grayson Steele was looking forward to a vacation with old friends. The vacation starts out perfect when he is seated next to a blond angel on the flight to Montana. He didn't expect to see her again or for her to jump into his car wearing a bloody wedding dress.

Will Grayson be able to help Kara untangle the lies of her past before it's too late? Or will an unexpected enemy take Kara from Grayson?

ABOUT AUTHOR

Linzi Baxter lives in Orlando, Florida with her husband and lazy basset hound. She started writing when voices inside her head wouldn't stop talking until the story was told. When not at work as an IT Manager, Linzi enjoys writing action-packed romances that will take you to the edge of your seat.

She enjoys engaging her readers with strong, interesting characters that have complex and stimulating stories to tell. If you enjoy a little (or maybe a whole lot) of steam and spice, don't miss checking out White Hat Security series.

When not writing, Linzi enjoys reading, watching college sports (GO UCF Knights), and traveling to Europe. She loves hearing from her readers and can't wait to hear from you!

Made in the USA
Monee, IL
14 January 2020